WILLOW

J.J. Maya

Book 2

In

The Beauty Shop Girl
Series

ISBN: 978-1-3999-4212-6

Cover illustration by Stephen McDermott

Book design by Socciones Editoria Digitale
www.socciones.co.uk

To my Mum, Stephen and Craig

CONTENTS

CHAPTER ONE

Tea at Tallulah's

I received a text from my old boss, Mrs. G. She asked me to meet her in Tallulah's Tearooms--one of the finer Upper East Side tea house establishments.

As I made my way through a busy throng of waiters and waitresses dressed in tailored black trousers accompanied by shiny black spats, I spotted her sitting in her customary ladylike repose, her toned legs displayed demurely beneath the round marble table, as the Mamas and Papas sang *Monday, Monday* through the sound system.

She called me over while one of the male waiters rushed to take my coat.

"Darling Willow," she said, peering at me over a pair of heavy, black-rimmed glasses, which she wore for show. "How the devil are you?"

"Oh . . . I'm fine, Mrs. G.--it's so great to see you again!" I responded.

"Just fine?" Mrs. G. raised an eyebrow, reminding me how to play this game. The perfectly perfunctory understated British response simply would not do.

"Just fabulous!" I gushed with faux excitement as I pulled the chair out and sat down opposite her.

"Then I'll cut to the chase and get straight to the point, shall I?" she smiled as she stirred her cup of peppermint tea, "Are you seeing anyone at the moment?"

Bloody hell! Why is she asking that? That's none of her business.

"Um," I stumbled, "Why do you want to know?" I held my breath.

Mrs. G. gave me one of her trademark looks while scanning me from head to toe.

"Just answer the question dear."

I shifted in my chair, trying to decide how much information I would reveal when the whole time I thought my personal status was none of her bloody business. Mrs. G just sat with her legs crossed--even her foot started to tap a little . . . impatience was oozing from every pore.

"Well." I cleared my throat. "I have been seeing Jake." I looked at her expression to see if there was the merest hint of recognition on her face.

"You do remember him, don't you?" I paused but her expression was blank.

"The guy you hired to do all the handyman jobs around D'Arcy's."

Mrs. G. took another sip of her tea. "Yes, I do recall." She pushed her glasses onto the top of her head.

Where is this conversation going and why did she bring me all the way over here? To discuss the intimate details of my personal life?

"Yes." Gigi Gerson nodded again. "Although I must admit . . . I was rather disappointed in your choice of men." Her eyes narrowed as she spoke.

Bloody hell! What is this?

My former boss appeared to do a mental calculation before gesturing to the waiter to bring the menu.

With full attention back on me, "Is it serious?" she inquired, staring hard at me, analysing me, making me think that everything depended on me answering her question correctly.

I hesitated. "Um... I suppose."

With disappointment writ large across her face, she pushed her teacup and saucer away.

"You don't sound too sure...I had hoped that you and Rick would have sorted things out . . . any likelihood of that happening?"

I sat back in the spindly chair and slammed the marble table in defiance. "Nope! Not a chance in hell!" I declared, trying to sound more resilient than I felt.

"I see." She tapped her painted pearlescent pink lower lip with her manicured finger. "Well. In that case . . ." Mrs. G. leaned down and pulled a large Manila envelope from her orange leather Hermes bag. She slid the envelope across the table, all the while holding my gaze. "I'd like you to read this." She got up to leave. "I'll be back in twenty minutes . . . I have an appointment with my interior designer." She looked at me. "I'll expect your answer when I return."

Whatever was in this envelope, she meant business.

"OK." I nodded, "I'll look over this while you're gone."

I sat on and watched her as she left the tearooms, the woman who did jail time for harbouring illegal immigrants in her old luxury Queens department store strode out of Tallulah's like the grande dame of New York society.

I was perplexed but also curious. As soon as she was out of sight, I quickly tore the envelope open and gasped as I read the contents. Mrs. G. had presented me with a contract. She wanted me to leave my position as a Chanel Makeup Artist at Barney's and work with her again!

The twenty minutes passed in a flash as I read and reread the document. My stomach flipped cartwheels as I took in all the details.

On her return, I looked on as she summoned the waiter to our table. In typical Mrs. G. fashion, she hadn't bothered to ask me if I was accepting the contract.

"Can you please take this awful tea away and bring us a nice, chilled bottle of Bolly?" She smiled over at me as she spoke. "I think we have something to celebrate?"

I couldn't contain my excitement any longer. I leaped up and hugged her.

"I think we do!"

I was trembling with self-doubt but did my best to conceal my nerves.

I knew that if I appeared hesitant, my boss would whisk this opportunity away from me.

The waiter soon arrived back at our table with a tray containing a bottle of champagne in an ice bucket and two crystal flutes. After the drinks had been poured, and he had departed, Mrs. G. and I clinked glasses.

"This is so much better than that awful peppermint tea, isn't it?" she smiled. "I don't know why anyone on earth wants to drink that foul stuff."

"But," I spluttered, "you always had a cup of it on your office desk at D'Arcy's!" I wondered what had brought on the change of heart. "I thought you loved that tea?"

Mrs. G. drew me a wicked grin, "So you never noticed the empty gin bottles in the trash?"

My mouth hung open. *What the?*

"It was all a disguise, darling!" Mrs. G. laughed. "I had to do something to get through the day." She grew serious as I started to protest. "Once I lost the store, I gave it up." she smacked the table. "Anyway, they don't allow alcohol in jail."

"Bloody hell! You kept that well-hidden."

"I was just the same as you dear--trying to keep it all together." She scrutinised me from head to toe as she spoke.

I looked at her in astonishment. I had no idea. Jake had hinted at a drinking problem but I didn't believe him.

Not my boss. Not my Mrs. G.

But then again, he had been the one clearing away the trash at the end of the day.

"OK. Now let's get down to business." She picked up her elegant Tiffany Blue pen. "Now. I'm sure you are already aware that D'Arcy's Department Store is in the hands of the Receivers?"

I had heard through the grapevine that this was the case.

I nodded. "Yes. I did hear that."

I guess she felt relieved to get that off her chest, and this was my cue to put the glass down and pull out the contract.

Mrs. G. had her copy laid out on the table in front of her. All at once, her lighthearted tone became serious and businesslike.

"As you can see from the document in front of you," she paused and looked at me, "I intend to launch a collection of pop-up beauty boutiques in several cities around the world. I have secured several leases in prime retail spots."

I always knew Mrs. G. had her head screwed on.

"If you agree to the terms, I want you to fly out to San Francisco and open up my West Coast boutique." She stared at me, gauging my reaction.

Inside, I was bursting with excitement.

She went on, "You'll be in charge of recruiting and hiring staff . . . getting the pop-up stores up and running. Got that?"

I nodded.

"Once you've accomplished that, you'll be flying to the U.K. to open up the London flagship store then you'll return to New York for the grand launch."

I nodded and grinned--I couldn't speak, afraid I would lose whatever cool I had.

"You're going to have to work very hard, Willow. I've invested the remainder of my family's fortune in this idea." Her tone darkened further. "I'm hoping the venture will be successful enough for me to buy D'Arcy's back but if this doesn't work out . . . I'm finished." She stared at me.

A wave of anxiety swept over me as I took on board the gravity of the situation--this was a heavy burden that I was about to accept. It was a lofty goal but one that meant a huge deal to my boss.

Holy crap! Am I even capable of this? She's trusting me with the remainder of the family fortune. If I screw up, she . . . no . . . we . . . lose everything!

Take the job and worry about it later. You can do this. She wouldn't have asked you if she didn't think you were capable. Don't be a wimp. Say Yes!

"So, what are you going to call this new venture?" I asked, hoping to distract Mrs. G., and anyway, the opportunity was too big and exciting to decline, of that I was absolutely sure.

"Plane Jane Beauty." She said, her voice was bold and confident.

I see she's thought about it.

"Plane as in the aircraft," she smiled. "And all the beauty consultants will be dressed as Flight Attendants." She turned and smiled at me. "Just like I did in the old days."

"Seriously?" I almost spat out my champagne. I knew that Mrs. G. had been an air hostess in her younger days but this was taking the biscuit.

"I spoke with my designer, and she is going to draw the layout of the boutiques like the interior of an airplane."

Has she gone completely bonkers? I wondered.

"Pardon the pun, but are you *on board* with the idea?" Mrs. G. erupted into peals of laughter.

"I guess I am. It's different . . ." I nodded, hoping to look like I meant it. "It has a certain *je ne sais quoi* about it." I didn't know what else to say. If truth be known, I thought she was going slightly looper in her old age. She went on, "It's a tribute to the golden years of flying when we flight attendants were admired and respected for our skills. We're going to keep the operation neat and petite, keep costs low and I'll be expecting you to gain the most 'bang for my buck' so to speak. I want you to use all your hard-won experience and do me proud."

As I drained my flute, I felt a heavy weight of responsibility rest on my shoulders. But still. I raised my empty glass to hers.

"You can bank on me, Gigi!"

Oh my God! I just called her by her first name.

"So, you are accepting my offer?" she asked, her left brow rising in anticipation.

It was the first time I had ever had the nerve to use her first name.

I think I've gotten away with it.

"Yes. I am." The bold words trundled out of my mouth.

"Another bottle of Bolly, Willow? We must toast your new position." Mrs. G. looked relieved.

"Yes. That would be perfect." I smiled, shaking inside, doing my best to hide my nerves, "What will my title be?"

"Officially?" she fluffed her hair. "COO--Chief Operations Officer."

I sat back in my chair and straightened my back, crossed my legs, and placed my palms on my lap.

"That sounds very *important*." I declared, not quite taking on board the significance of it all.

"Now, don't allow yourself to get too hung up on titles." She shuffled the papers together and shoved her belongings back into the Hermes bag. "At the end of the day, you are my right-hand woman, my person on the ground, my trouble-shooter, my eyes, and ears--get the picture?"

I nodded in agreement while running the title over and over in my head. "Willow Campbell-Delgado, Head of Operations, Plane Jane Beauty!"

Mrs. G. pulled a small white card out of her purse.

"Here." She handed the card to me. "Take this. This is my marketing man's details . . . his name is George, and he'll be looking after the PR & Promotions."

"Thanks."

"Oh! Before I forget. Your married name! Is it still Campbell-Delgado or will it be changing back . . . You know, when your divorce comes through?"

I tensed up. I hadn't considered my legal name up until this point. Mrs. G. saw that I visibly flinched on hearing her question.

"I'm sorry to ask, only I need to know what to put on the paperwork." She eyed me intently.

"I'll be Campbell-Delgado for the foreseeable future. I expect the divorce will be through in the next few months."

"That's fine. I'll let the lawyers know to expect a name change. It's no big deal."

I flinched again. *It is to me! It's a bloody huge deal. I didn't marry Rick Delgado only to divorce him a year later.*

"Oh! Wait! " Mrs. G. delved into the bag one more time. She pulled out a thin envelope. "You'll need this." She leaned over and handed me the envelope. Before I could open it, she said, "Inside, you'll find your flight ticket and a company credit card. I want you packed and ready to fly out tomorrow afternoon . . . and I want a receipt for everything."

She put a lot of emphasis on the word *everything*.

I hesitated, "But what about my notice period at Barney's?"

"Don't worry too much about that, darling, the store manager and I go way back. I'll speak to her."

"Right." I nodded. "OK then."

I couldn't stop grinning and nodding.

Stop it, Willow! Be professional! Act like butter wouldn't melt.

I was giddy with excitement. I cleared my voice. "So, do you have a uniform in mind for this position?" I asked, my thoughts racing at the current state of my laundry.

"As a matter of fact, I do." Mrs. G. pulled out her iPad. "Glad you asked."

She showed me a selection of flight attendants dressed in uniform, including one of herself in her younger days when she flew with Pan Am.

"Wait," I raised a brow, "You want me to dress like that? Wear a neck scarf and a tippy hat. While I'm working?"

"Yes. I do. I want all staff to adhere to cabin crew style rules and regulations . . . just like we did back then. I want long hair in buns and I want nails to match the lipstick. I want sheer pantyhose and heeled shoes for walking to and from work, and low-heeled shoes to wear behind the counter. I want white blouses matched with pencil skirts and tailored jackets set off with a scarf tied at the neck."

I was sorry I had asked but I understood exactly what she was trying to achieve. A distinctive 'Plane Jane Beauty' brand.

"This is all very smart . . . will we get the makeup artists to adhere to these strict guidelines?" I regretted asking the question as soon as I opened my mouth.

"That--my dear--is your job." Mrs. G. indicated for the waiter to bring her coat as she downed the last dregs of champagne. "Now. I must go home." She stopped and gave me a lingering glance. "I know you'll do me proud, Willow." She reached over to pat my shoulder. "Call me if you need me but don't expect me to answer straight away--there is other business to attend to."

And then she was off, heading into the bright lights of the city streets.

I understood the last sentence was for the benefit of those sitting around us. She was still keeping up appearances no matter which hand life dealt her. I knew that Mrs. G. no longer had a glamorous pad to head home to, or much in the way of business to attend to. I had heard she was living in a tiny apartment in Jackson Heights, and she had confessed that she had sunk all her family's wealth into this latest venture.

Later that evening, as I let myself into my own small apartment in Hell's Kitchen, I noticed a card had been slid under the doorjamb. I bent down and picked it up, recognizing the handwriting--Jake.

Shit! What does he want?

In an instant, the buzzer went off. I could tell from the security camera that it was him. And he was carrying a bunch of flowers.

Bloody hell. Must be coming to apologise for last night's argument. That's all I need.

We had been an item for almost a year now but lately, well, we just didn't seem to be getting on.

I buzzed him in then scurried around the apartment picking up pieces of stray laundry. I hated having unannounced guests. I did a quick scan to see if everything was in its place before reapplying my Chanel Pirate lipstick and spraying the last remaining drops of Terre over me.

I noticed the envelope with the paperwork sticking out of my Kate Spade and quickly stuffed it inside. I wasn't yet ready to spring my good news on him. Not while I was still trying to digest everything for myself. The afternoon champagne had left me feeling tipsy--all I wanted to do was take a nap and think about my big career move, not entertain an uninvited boyfriend.

Jake bundled into the apartment, smiling and handing me a bouquet of rustic out-of-season carnations. The flowers did nothing for me but I had to give him 10 out of 10 for effort. He leaned in and kissed me, while I pulled away.

"What's the matter with you?" he asked in his lilting Irish brogue. "You're not still mad at me, are you?"

"And if I am, would that be a problem?" I asked, running the cold tap while trying to find a vase to put the flowers in. In my rush to avoid him, I accidentally dropped it on the kitchen floor, spilling water and scattering broken glass everywhere.

"Shit!" I stepped over the mess, trying my best not to stand on shards of glass.

"Have you been drinking?"

I turned and gave him the stink eye.

"You have, haven't you?" he goaded, increasing my temper.

He stood watching me, arms folded, berating me as I mopped the floor. "So what happened to the no-midweek alcohol rule? That didn't last long, did it?"

I exhaled loudly. *Here we bloody go again!*

"Do you want coffee?" I snapped. Switching on the kettle while scouring around for another vase. I hated his carnations. They were beige and brown and rustic gold. I was a pink peony girl, but he would never understand that. I took the ugly flowers and thrust them into a cheap orange plastic vase.

"Nah. I don't want your coffee." He turned away with that classic *I'm in a huff* expression that I despised.

I placed the messy flower arrangement on top of the sideboard and stood back, pretending to admire them.

"Now. Don't these look nice?" I knew I was being a bitch but just couldn't help my sarcastic tone.

The orange and gold colour display looked ridiculous up against my Farrow and Ball Sap Green walls. The man just didn't get it.

Jake shrugged and walked away. He got that his presence irritated me.

Ten minutes later, we both sat on the purple velvet couch in silence. I wracked my brain, trying to figure out how to broach the subject of me leaving town while Jake continued to brood.

"So where were you this afternoon?" he asked. "Did you go out drinking with the girls from work again?"

I stared at him for a moment.

"Nope!" I shook my head.

Best tell him, Willow.

I took a sip of wine from my favourite pink mug.

"Did you think anymore about what I said the other night?" he asked, staring hard at me.

I played dumb.

"What was that?"

Now it was Jake's turn to sigh. "Moving in with me? Like we discussed."

"No. I haven't given it much thought." I stared at my nails. *Must fit in a manicure at the airport if I can.*

Jake appeared deflated. "Oh. I see."

I felt sorry for him. But I didn't agree with his argument about me giving up my hard-won Hell's Kitchen apartment to move upriver with him, just to save on utility bills. It was hardly what I would call a romantic proposal.

He clocked my favourite self-help book lying across the arm of the winged armchair.

"Did you go to a café and read your yellow book?" he asked, clutching at conversation.

This must be torture for him.

I placed my coffee mug down on the side table, stood up, and fetched my bag.

"If you must know, I went to Tallulah's to meet with Gigi Gerson."

Jake began to tap his fingers on the side of the couch. He did this when he was nervous or frustrated.

I pulled out the large envelope and handed it to him.

"Here. Read this."

"What's this?" he asked, staring up at me.

"A contract," I stated. I folded my arms in defiance and stood looming above him as he began to scan the document. After a few moments, he stuffed the paper back into the envelope. There were no peals of excitement or bouts of congratulations.

Instead, he simply said, "You're going to be gone for months at a time?"

I nodded but kept silent.

"What about me?" he looked at me and shrugged. "Where do I fit into all of this?" A frown descended on his brow.

I didn't know what to say!

Jake stared right through me, causing my steel-like resolve to bend.

"It'd be nice if you could say something like 'Congratulations, Willow', or something to that effect."

But the moment had already passed. If he said it now, it would mean nothing.

Jake fetched his coat. He turned his back to me and threw one arm into the coat sleeve, then turned and stared at me.

"My babies. I thought you were going to have my kids. All this time, we've been together, Willow. What a waste of time! What a damn waste of time and energy."

Now it was my turn to be gobsmacked. *His kids?! When did we ever talk about babies?*

Jake opened the door and made to leave.

"We're done, Willow." He slammed the door behind him.

I threw myself down on the couch and exhaled. Did he break up with me? I couldn't believe it. It was supposed to be the other way around. I sighed with relief.

Now it was time to celebrate! I walked into the kitchen and poured a 'consolatory' glass of wine. *He just dumped me?! He wanted me to have his kids!*

I always knew deep down that Jake wanted to be settled and have children. I was thankful for his help but did I owe him years of marriage and motherhood? If I was ever going to marry again then it had to be with the right man, a man I was head over heels in love with. I thought that man was Rick but I soon saw the writing on the wall . . .

I guessed I had done Jake a favour, he could move on now and find someone who wanted the same things he did. I caught my reflection in the window. My complexion looked lighter. I lifted my glass. *Cheers!* I smiled. I knew I had made the right decision.

CHAPTER TWO

Pink Peony Girl

As the wheels of the aircraft skidded along the runway at SFO International Airport, I pressed my face up close to the window and peered out. It was raining. San Francisco had always been on my list of places to visit, so I didn't let the weather dampen my mood.

I collected my luggage from the carousel and strolled along the terminal in my leopard print kitten heels. A memory of walking onto the beauty hall floor at Devonshire's Department Store quickly flew into my mind.

Grumpy Greta--my then Department Manager--had just approached me with a list of impossible-to-reach sales targets, setting me up--as she liked to do--for failure.

I always knew she had it in for me.

If only she could see me now! Off to open up a brand-new boutique in one of the most fashionable areas of the city! "Believe you are and you will be," I murmured under my breath as Sammy Davis Jr. belted out the lyrics to *Mr. Bojangles* on the airport sound system. 'Believe you are and you will be' was a phrase from my little yellow book that had always struck me.

As I walked towards 'Baggage Reclaim,' I remembered how Jackson--my best friend and colleague from D'Arcy's--urged me to come out from behind the beauty counter and to start making my own luck in life.

"He was right", I thought. It's up to me to reach out and grab every opportunity that comes my way. I felt like I was on cloud nine, as I stood in line outside 'Arrivals'--the sun was beginning to break through the clouds and I could feel the heat of the Californian sunshine beating down on me.

Jackson. Where are you?

I recalled the immigration officer telling me how all illegal aliens were deported to the point of origin.

If only I could find some way of getting in contact with him . . .

The cab finally pulled up. I got in and handed a card with the hotel's address to the cabbie. He smiled back at me. "Lombard Street."

I threw myself back in the leather seat as the driver drove out of the parking lot, and we sped off towards the city centre.

Thirty-five minutes later, I switched on the kettle in the small but up-to-the-minute galley kitchen on the 14th floor of my hotel, overlooking the famous squiggly Lombard Street with the majestic Golden Gate Bridge off in the distance. As I took in my surroundings, I was surprised that Mrs. G. was sparing no expense to ensure my comfort and safety on this trip, and for that I was grateful, knowing full well how fragile her finances were.

I unpacked my 'airline' edition uniform, hanging it up in the bathroom, thinking that the steam from my evening shower would erase the wrinkles. I opened up two sachets of artisan coffee granules the hotel provided and poured the boiling water into my cup while looking around.

The room was a bit on the small side but housed an oversized sage green velvet armchair not too different from the one that Jackson liked to slink into in his New York apartment. I made a mental note to thank my boss for putting me up in such stylish accommodation. Just then my phone buzzed. It was Jake.

"Shit!" I jumped, spilling hot coffee on my arm and hand. I didn't feel like taking his call but thought I'd better pick up.

"Willow! Thank God you picked up!" he gasped. "I gotta go home--back to Ireland."

"What's happened?" I asked, carefully placing the cup down on the side table.

"It's Jules. My brother. I'm on my way to the airport . . . he's been in a motorbike accident."

My stomach lurched.

"I'm not going to make it back in time Willow--I just know it. I--" The line went dead.

Great. I checked my connection--no service.

I'm useless. *Poor Jake!* A text message arrived a second later.

I guess my service is back.

I looked down at the message and swallowed.

It read: WILL YOU JOIN ME? JULES WOULD HAVE LOVED YOU, WILLOW.

I felt terrible. Jake was tugging at my heartstrings and the old Willow--the people pleaser--would have booked a ticket and flown to Ireland, but not this Willow. He had broken up with me. Besides, I reasoned, there was no way in hell Mrs. G. is going to give me time off to go. I just know it.

The hotel room phone rang--*back to the here and now*--I sighed.

"Hello?" It was the reception desk calling up. "A visitor?" I wrinkled my brows. "For me? But I'm not expecting anyone." I racked my brain, trying to remember if Mrs. G. had said anything about a visitor. "No." I shook my head. "Don't send him up." I pulled on my coat while talking to the receptionist. "I'll be right down."

I was very big on hotel safety and didn't want strangers turning up at my door, so I closed the door behind me and made my way to the elevator.

Who can it be?

I stepped out of the lift and made my way toward the reception desk.

Rick stood opposite me.

"What the hell are you doing here?" I frowned.

"What kind of welcome is that? He leaned in for a tight hug not giving me a chance to step away.

I pushed him back. "How did you know I was here?"

"I bumped into Mrs. G. outside that Tallulah's place you girls like, and she told me she had sent you here to open up a boutique. Just so happens my business was sending me here too!" He smiled as the heady scent of Vetiver hit my nostrils.

"I don't believe a word of this-but come with me." I indicated for him to follow.

I led him toward the elevator. The mirrored interior showed us from every angle. My hands made fists as we rode in silence and my insides were rolling with nerves as I let us into the room. Rick chewed a finger-nail.

Is he as nervous as me?

I looked on as he scanned the room. He blew a low whistle.

"Gigi's busting out her bank balance for this dump?" he smirked.

"Dump? Ha! This place? Much better than your apartment!"

Rick stepped closer, attempting to hug me once more. "You were al-ways the pragmatic one, weren't you?"

"I had no choice but to be like that." I shrugged. "Coffee?" I asked, rushing to the kitchen. "Do you want one sachet or two?"

"No thanks," he made a face. "Drank it all the way over on the flight."

"What?" I asked in mock horror. "No champagne for you?"

Rick looked uncharacteristically shy. "Had a little too much of the stuff the night before." He chuckled, looking pleased with himself too.

He picked up the phone receiver, "But I'm sober now . . . hang on, I'll call room service. They do offer room service, don't they?" he asked, flipping through the flimsy menu.

"Don't be so snobby. Of course, they do. I'm checked in here for a few weeks, so I'm hoping they do."

He put his finger up to his mouth to shush me.

"Hey," Rick shouted into the receiver. "Send up a bottle of your best champagne, please!"

"No, don't!" I called out.

I tried to grab the phone off him, but he turned his back on me. "And we'll order two servings of fries." He smirked as I stood in defiance, with both hands on hips.

Why does he need to do this? All this time, and he's still trying to impress me?

Rick threw a $100 bill down on the desk.

"Champagne and chips! What are you playing at?"

With signature aplomb, he threw himself down on the armchair, smiling at me.

"So," he looked me up and down, "what's been happening with my favourite wife?"

I hated how he liked to jest about our marital state.

"Are you still dating that country bumpkin, what's his name? Jack?" he asked, a sneer appearing across his complexion.

"Jake. You know full well his name is Jake." I brushed invisible crumbs off the top of the bed. "And he's not a country bumpkin! He's a nice man--a very nice man."

"That says it all, *nice!*"

I didn't like how he emphasized the word.

"I mean who in hell wants to be described as nice?" he smirked.

"Well, that's something you'll never have to worry about!" I stuck my tongue out, unpacking while he talked.

"So, where is he?" He asked, looking around the room for signs of another man.

"Um . . ." I hesitated. "We're not together anymore, he dumped me before I flew out here."

Rick smacked the armrest, "Best bloody news I've heard all day!"

What's he so pleased about?

"He was never the right guy for you, babe."

That got my back up.

"Don't call me that! I'm not your *babe*," I reminded him.

"Sorry." Rick shrugged.

Doesn't look that sorry to me.

***

The room service attendant saved us with a knock at the door. The champagne and fries had arrived.

"Go easy on that fizz, Rick!"

I held my hand over the brim of the glass so that he couldn't refill the slender flute for the third time. "I have work tomorrow morning and I'm not going in with a hangover," I stated, staring at him like I meant business.

"WOW!" His eyes widened like he was seeing me for the first time. "You've changed!" I remembered how Rick and I could swig whisky and champagne back at his apartment on Ingram Street in Glasgow like there was no tomorrow. But there is a tomorrow.

"Yes." I nodded. "I think I have." I raised my glass.

Rick appeared meek like he realised he was the cause of the change in my life.

"I'm really proud of you, Willow." He stared at me, while he spoke. "You've made some real progress in your job. I mean look at you!" He smiled as he held his arms out wide. "Living the high life! Jetting all over the world, opening up beauty boutiques! My shy little Willow."

I had to agree with him. Even the yellow book could not foretell the dizzying heights my career would reach in such a short time.

"Of course. It's all because of me." A smug look reached across his features.

I rolled my eyes.

The old arrogant Rick is back.

19

"Really? How do you figure?" I asked, holding his gaze, refusing to be intimidated.

"Well." He strutted, walking around the place as he owned it. "If I hadn't walked into Devonshire's that fateful day and seen you behind your counter, reading your yellow book, you wouldn't be sitting with me right now in this Californian high-rise."

I laughed. I laughed so hard.

"So, I get no credit for all the years of hard work standing behind the makeup counter, going to night school after working all day? I work my way up the ladder yet . . . Somehow, this success is all down to you?" I set my glass on the table in front of me and crossed my arms. "You know it's about time you offloaded your saviour mentality."

How the hell did I end up with him?

But my thoughts were drowned out by a moving sensation underfoot, coupled with the strangest sound of coat hangers clattering together in the wardrobe. The contents of my glass bubbled over, spilling onto the carpet as I stared at Rick. He was ashen-faced.

"What the fuck was that?" he asked but before I could answer, it happened again--the same sickening movement underfoot.

"I think it was a tremor."

"What do we do, Willow?" he frantically searched my eyes, the colour draining from his tanned complexion. I had never seen him look so petrified.

"How the hell do I know?" I screeched, panic rising in my voice as the clanging noise grew more violent.

Rick gripped me.

Think, Willow! Think!

I racked my memory trying to remember films I had seen, where people went through emergency drills. Instinctively, I understood what to do in the event of a hurricane and tsunami, but an earthquake? Do we run into the street? Or do we stay here and hide? *Shit!*

You should have read the earthquake instructions on the back of the hotel room door, Willow.

Scanning the room, looking for somewhere big enough for both of us to hide, I saw that Rick had grabbed the champagne bottle from the ice bucket and began to consume the contents.

"Nice one!" I smirked. "Very helpful."

He clutched my hand and led me towards the walk-in wardrobe, chugging the bottle as he went.

"If I'm gonna die, then I'm gonna die happy," he stated.

Closing the wardrobe door behind us, darkness washed over us as the floor beneath us lolled.

"Give me that damn bottle!" I demanded, slugging the fizz back so fast that the bubbles went straight up my nostrils.

"Jesus, Willow. Slow the fuck down."

How long will this go on?

I handed it back to him as the rattling of the clothes hangers slowly began to dissipate. The siren stopped wailing.

I took a deep breath, as I attempted to calm my heart rate.

As if on cue, the phone in my pocket went off. I knew it would be Jake. He would know about the tremors by now, but I dared not answer.

I mean how could I possibly explain that I was standing in a dark wardrobe drinking emergency champagne with my soon-to-be ex-husband?

Petrified and too scared to move, I concentrated on my breathing while keeping my eyes closed until the phone stopped ringing.

Seizing the moment--as usual--Rick leaned in and clasped his hands around my waist.

"God, I missed you." He breathed on my neck as he pulled me in tighter. "I'm so sorry for treating you the way I did . . ." he whispered. "I fucked up--I know I did."

I stepped away so that I could face him in the darkness.

I placed my fingers on his rough lips, urging him to be quiet. "*Shh. Listen.*"

The vibrations had subsided, while an eerie silence descended upon us.

"Do you think it's safe to open the door?" I asked, fumbling in the dark trying to find the door handle.

"I think we should stay here a few moments longer," Rick suggested, as he guided my hand to his crotch. "At least until everything calms down."

Right on cue, my phone burst into life. "Saved by the bell," I said. Rick threw his arms up as I took the call.

"Yes." I paused. "I'm OK." I cupped the receiver of the phone and mouthed, "it's Jake" to silence Rick. "Yes . . . it was scary . . . no. I'm alone." I lied and looked at Jake, begging him to stay quiet. "I'm standing in the walk-in wardrobe--apparently it's the safest place to be." I looked at Rick as he stepped out of the wardrobe, gathered up his belongings, and made for the door.

I looked on as he opened the door to my hotel room, he indicated that he would call me, and then he left.

"No." I continued talking as I stared at the door. "I'm sorry Jake. I don't expect I will be flying over, but I wish you and your family all the best." I added, feeling like a dirtbag for exactly two seconds. "Goodbye, Jake."

As I put the phone back in my pocket, I threw myself on top of the bed. *I'm a mess.*

I took out the yellow book and opened at a random chapter--"Physical attractions are common, but a mental connection is rare."

Did I ever have a mental connection with Rick or Jake? Or had I fallen for looks? You can do better, Willow. So much better. Girl, this is your opportunity to prove yourself, don't let these men mess with your emotions.

CHAPTER THREE

Sassy in San Francisco

After all the drama of my arrival in San Francisco, I decided to go out and explore before it got too late. I threw on my favourite springtime coat, the one I had bought with my first pay cheque from D'Arcy's Department Store. After going through a few East Coast winters, it was nice to be able to discard the layers.

I left the hotel room and made my way down the 14 flights of stairs. It felt safer that way. After that experience, the last thing I wanted was to be trapped in an elevator during a second tremor.

Six minutes later and feeling dizzy, I walked past the same concierge from earlier.

"Madam! Is everything OK?" He looked concerned for my well-being. "You look a little flushed."

"Yes, everything's fine . . . I think . . ." I started to walk away but turned back. "It's just that, well this is going to sound silly, but the coat hangers were bashing against each other and," I let out a small laugh, "I got a fright and decided not to take the elevator but to walk down the stairs instead." I held onto the back of the reception desk chair. "All 14 flights." My legs wobbled like jelly while my head spun.

The concierge laughed, then asked, "Is this your first time in San Francisco?"

"Yes." I nodded. "Why?"

"Well, I think you just experienced one of our famous tremors."

"You mean it was an actual earthquake?" I thought I was going to faint.

"Not so much an earthquake, more like a little rumble." He smirked.

I puckered my lips. I didn't like him one bit. *Little rumble, huh?*

"Oh, it's nothing to worry about. I assure you." He scribbled on a piece of paper and then handed it to me. "If you are concerned, then you can download this app on your phone --that'll keep you advised about the next time the earth will shake." He let out a small self-satisfied laugh.

"What a wanker," I mumbled under my breath and walked out, grabbing the piece of paper from him. I saw he had scrawled his number on the back.

Yuck!

I crumpled it up and threw it in the nearest trash bin.

I strolled down Lombard Street, inhaling the sights and sounds of the city while taking in the activities of the locals, who, as far as I could see, neither looked up nor down regarding the whole 'moving earth' scenario.

Perhaps they are used to the earth shaking and I will just have to be on board with it too.

***

The local bars, restaurants, and coffee houses were quickly filling up with workers who were finishing their shifts and looking to enjoy some spring downtime.

I spotted a small group sitting at a table on the sidewalk patio area of a local bar. After the fright I just had, I decided a stiff drink was in order.

Hmm. Brodie's Bar, I read the menu hanging above the bar.

I entered the bar and took in the rustic-chic surroundings: the bar top looked like it was constructed from driftwood, lending a beachy, breezy ambiance to the place. I felt relaxed as famous songs from the 1960s played in the background. The bar area was lined with industrial copper shelves set against a driftwood-clad wall, and the wall lighting cast a dim glow over the copper, creating a feeling of instant warmth.

What will I order? I pondered as the bartender ignored me. *I wish I wasn't alone. Bad enough walking in on my own.* I looked around, impatiently tapping the sharp end of my company credit card on the counter.

A large group of rowdy office workers barged in and made straight to the front of the bar area, jostling me out of position.

"Hey! Look where you're going!" I called out.

Bloody cheek!

I got that traveling the world as a lone businesswoman was going to throw up its own unique set of challenges. I had to stand my ground.

I'll be damned if I'm going to be holed up alone in my hotel room every night.

I mustered up an ounce of courage coupled with my newly acquired New York street smarts and shouted above the noise.

"Hey! I was here first!" My voice sounded louder than I wanted it to be.

The office workers stopped their chitchat.

"Hey Pat," one of them yelled, "this young lady was first."

I looked over to find out who was backing me up.

"Young!" I said, smiling. "Pushing 33 and still being called *young*! My devotion to top-tier skincare must be paying off." I continued to tap the credit card for added effect as the blonde-haired bartender continued to ignore me.

"What do you have to do to get some service around here?" I mumbled under my breath.

The barman swaggered over in my direction.

"How about being polite?" he stared at me, unblinking. "We're short-staffed today."

"I see that," I shrugged. "I'm just not used to being ignored." The words came flying out of my mouth before I realised what I was saying.

Willow! Such sass! The voice in my head reprimanded me.

"Well, well, well," Pat leaned over, "OK then." He smirked. "What can I get you?"

"What do you recommend?" I asked.

"How about 'sex on the beach?" He shot me a cheeky smile, causing me to blush. "Or if you've got a sweet tooth, then you've got to try our famous Chocolate Martini made with Ghirardelli chocolate."

"Perfect. I'll have one of those."

"One Chocolate Martini coming up." He drew me a wry smile.

So full of himself.

I stared around the bar as I waited, casting a sideways glance at the barman.

I watched as he ran his fingers through his hair, while he poured the drink into the glass.

Looks like he's got the hots for himself. Freakin' loves himself.

I waited. I'd had it up to here with men and this one was no different.

"One Chocolate Martini coming up." Came the droll reply. He turned his back on me and walked towards the lineup of liquor bottles on the shelf. I noticed his jeans were falling off his backside and his pale blue bowling shirt was only half-tucked in.

Needs to smarten himself and his attitude. Way too old to be rockin' a quiff. Could do with a few lessons in customer service too . . .

A chill ran down my spine as my phone pinged to life. I knew it would be Jake. I decided not to look.

The worker from earlier held out his hand to shake mine as Pat delivered my drink. I noted Pat's gaze lingered as the man shook my hand, I guess from his standpoint behind the bar he had seen this move many times.

"The name's Charlie."

"Willow," I said. "Willow Campbell-Delgado but about to return to Campbell." I regretted my words as soon as they escaped from my mouth. *Why on earth did I say that?*

Michael Bublé was belting out *It's a new day and a new dawn* on the sound system as I caught the bartender glance over again.

"Such cold hands," Charlie replied, smiling, his blue eyes glittering bright under the dusky lighting.

"Everyone says that," I replied. "Makeup Artist hands." I plastered a fake smile across my face.

"Makeup Artist? Well, O.K.! That's different." He turned his body to face me. "So what brings you to San Fran?" Charlie asked, staring at me with his full attention.

"How do you know I'm not from here?" I asked, sipping on the cold cocktail. *Way too much ice.* I narrowed my eyes at Pat.

"That Scottish accent is a bit of a giveaway, is it not?" He smiled but I didn't smile back.

My phone pinged again. I knew that Jake was waiting for me to respond.

"Oh . . ." I grimaced. "Work." I waved a hand looking at my cell phone. I reached out and squeezed his shoulder. "Would you excuse me? I must take this."

I stepped out of the bar onto the busy pavement and dialed Jake's number. Just as expected, he answered straight away.

"Willow. Are you coming over? Yes or No? I need to know."

"Oh, Jake. You dumped me. Remember? No. I'm not flying over to visit your brother in the hospital."

I felt bad. Lousy for allowing myself to be chatted up by Charlie whom no doubt had a gullible Charlotte patiently waiting for him at home.

Charlie homed in on me as soon as I stepped back into the bar.

"I bought you another drink." He said, smiling at me while attempting to hand me the cocktail.

Shit! Here we go . . .

I waved my hand in front of him to let him know that I didn't want to take his cocktail. *God only knows what might be in that glass.* I had heard of so many horror stories of roofies being dropped into girls' drinks, there was no way I was taking a chance with this complete stranger.

"Thanks, but no thanks," I stated. "I've got a big workload tomorrow."

I took a step back from him, trying my best to procure some space between us, but he was having none of it. He stepped forward and placed his hand on the base of my spine. I shuddered with disgust and quickly flicked his hand away.

"What's the matter?" he asked in a high voice like he wasn't used to the big brush-off.

"Absolutely nothing is the matter with me," I replied in a haughty voice, shaking my head. "Now would you excuse me, please?" A small roar went up as his cohorts gathered around to see Charlie being ditched.

I walked back towards the bar and left a bunch of dollars as a tip.

"Is he bothering you?" the barman asked, tea towel over one shoulder and pen behind his ear. "Don't let him annoy you, he tries it on with every good-looking female who crosses his path."

"I don't know quite how to take that," I stated.

"Take what?" he looked confused.

"The good-looking part," I said. "Is that supposed to be a compliment?"

Patrick shook his head, sighed, and puffed his cheeks out. "You got me confused lady . . . are you one of those feminist types that can't take a compliment?"

"That sentence is so loaded." I narrowed my eyes.

This is way too much like hard work.

"Look, I'm only trying to help and save you from that douchebag, but if you think you can handle him then so be it." Pat walked off, shoving the bunch of dollars back at me. "You can keep your lousy tip," he said. "I don't want it." He turned his attention to the line of bar dwellers who were waiting to be served. "Next," he called, drawing me a dirty look.

"I'm outta here," I spoke to myself as I turned and stormed past sleazy Charlie and his co-workers, making a mental note never to step foot in Brodie's Bar again.

Back in the hotel, I rushed past the lecherous concierge and made my way toward the elevator. *Earthquake or no earthquake there was no bloody way in hell I was walking up 14 flights of stairs.*

My first night in San Francisco had left me feeling harassed. Time to calm down and relax. I checked the time. It was 8:00 pm . . . Just time enough for a relaxing bath and meditation session before sleep.

My phone rang. It was Mrs. G.

"Willow! Did you check into your hotel?"

"Yes!" I tried to sound chirpy. "The views are out of this world." It was pitch dark and I couldn't see anything but twinkling street and skyscraper lights, but she didn't need to know that. "I'm sorry I didn't call--"

"OK dear." she interrupted. "Never mind all that, I arranged five interviews for you to conduct at the premises tomorrow morning."

This woman does not miss a beat!

"Excellent." I inhaled sharply, tapping my pen on the table.

Mrs. G. interrupted before I had the chance to ask any questions. "Now remember, you are the stand-in Manager until you hire a suitable candidate for the role--it is in your best interests to find the right person for the job as quickly as possible."

"Yes. I know." I sighed as I took in my surroundings. I wanted to get off the phone and chill out for a bit.

"I sent you an email confirming appointment times with names. We have some very qualified people in this group." I listened as she took a sharp intake of breath. "But always remember the hidden rule of retail."

What? What hidden rule of retail? What is she talking about?

"Go on . . ." I prompted.

"Don't make me say it, Willow." Her voice lowered as if to avoid being overheard.

My heart sank. I knew what she wanted me to do. *She wants me to hire based on looks.*

"You know fine well what I mean, dear." Mrs. G. sighed. "The uniforms I have ordered only go up to size 10."

Shit!

"But Mrs. G.!" I paused. "You can't make me employ people on looks and size alone!"

I stared at the handset in disbelief. My boss was gone--she had hung up on me.

I threw myself down on the armchair. She had just set me with the almost impossible task of finding a candidate who ticked all her boxes. Someone bright, beautiful, business savvy, and no bigger than a size 10 to boot.

I guess employment rules and regulations don't mean a thing to Mrs. G.

I lay down on top of the bed and stared at the ceiling, thoughts milling in and out of my mind at break-neck speed. *I need to draw a bath, stop thinking of the events of the day . . . stop thinking about Gigi and her endless demands.* I reached into my Kate Spade and fumbled around for a small silver tin containing one scented tea light.

Matches. I need matches. I'll be damned if I'm phoning that horrible concierge.

I searched my bag but there was none. Then I remembered I had taken a small pack from Brodie's Bar. It was a habit I had developed since arriving in New York--taking a box of matches from every bar I went into. A tiny souvenir and a snapshot of my new life in the Big Apple.

Ten minutes later, as I lay back in the warm water and stared at the stillness of the flame, my thoughts flickered back to the barman in Brodie's.

I mean, who in the hell does he think he is?

CHAPTER FOUR

Fully Crewed

The next morning, I awoke early to a stream of text messages from Jake, Mrs. G., and Rick. I ignored the texts from Rick and Jake and concentrated on the work-related ones. The interview process was due to start at 10:00 am sharp and would last until mid-afternoon.

As I drank my coffee, I surveyed the list of candidates and their CVs and made some notes in my agenda about who I thought might make the best employees for Mrs. G.'s west coast boutique. There were a few names that stuck out in my mind--notably Carmen, Josefina, and Finn.

I wondered how they might feel about the prospect of dressing up as flight attendants but decided I would tell them about that at the later stages of the interviewing process.

I placed my feet on the edge of the bed and sat back in the green-winged armchair. Yesterday's events left me feeling shell-shocked and I hoped that today would be better.

"I need to do some affirmations," I said to no one in particular. "Where's my yellow book?

"All lack and delay now crumble away," I said out loud.

I hoped and prayed that today would bring me the results--there was so much banking on me making a success of the venture for both my sake and my boss's.

"Now's the day to redeem myself." I placed the coffee cup in the galley kitchen and proceeded to get ready. It was a powerful red lipstick day, my flight attendant uniform had been hanging up in the bathroom overnight. The standards of appearance were set high--*sky-high*, so to speak.

30-minutes later, I was preened, primed, and ready to go. I had to hand it to my boss. The uniform made me feel good. It fits in all the right places and yet provided a certain ease of movement and comfort. I adorned my white shirt with a red, white, and blue neck-tie, and she had even supplied a set of ornate silver wings to be attached to the navy uniform jacket. The pencil skirt fits well in all the right places.

I checked myself out in the mirror.

Not bad Willow . . . not bad.

The Plane Jane ensemble suited me.

The pop-up was located on Beach Street, opposite Joseph Conrad Square near Fisherman's Wharf in North Harbor. It was in an iconic spot and would be leased for just six months--enough time to garner whether it would likely be a success. I observed from reading the lease that Mrs. G. had used her business kudos to negotiate a cut-price deal with the landlord. If the shop proved to be unsuccessful, she would simply lock up at the end of the contract and move on to a different location. Outside the hotel, I hailed a cab to the venue allocated for the interviewing process.

"Fisherman's Wharf, please!" I bounced into the back of the taxi.

Ten minutes later, the driver pulled up outside a rather grand-looking boutique, positioned to take advantage of footfall from nearby Ghirardelli Square. On one side of the pop-up store stood a historic Victorian-style hotel. It appeared to be popular with tourists as a constant stream of people entered and left the premises. On the other side of Plane Jane Beauty stood a charming Italian roast house.

Mrs. G. could not have picked a better spot for her new business venture.

I popped into the café and introduced myself to the owner, Fred. I asked him if I could open up a tab for my new hires. He appeared delighted at the news we were moving in. He informed me that the premises had been lying vacant for over a year.

That's strange! The shop would have been scooped up by a big retailer by now . . . Why would anyone leave this spot? It's prime real estate!

"How much do you want to spend on your staff?" Fred wielded his notebook and pen.

"I think $25 a day should be enough to cover it."

He laughed. "First time in the city?"

I blushed, "How can you tell?"

There goes my hard-won New York savvy.

"Well." Fred cleared his throat for maximum effect. "The average price for a cup of coffee in these parts is $7." He stated, leaning in on the polished wood counter. "How many staff members do you have?" He had a kindly, well-lived face-from years of hard graft and exposure to the Californian sunshine no doubt. His brown eyes shone as he spoke.

"Five--including myself. But I won't be staying, not permanently." I gave a small smile. "I'm only here to get the store up and running."

"That's a pity." Fred winked as he looked me up and down. "I was kinda hoping you would be hanging out for a bit."

I blushed again.

Dang! So not used to so much male attention. What's with the men in San Francisco?

Fred continued, "You gonna feed them too?"

"Yes." I cleared my throat. "At least, I am hoping to. A coffee and a snack? For each person for five days a week."

Fred scribbled in his notebook and then showed me the calculation.

"That's going to be $250 a week."

I gasped. Mrs. G. had been insistent that I feed my staff as she said it fostered good employer/employee relations-but I don't think she reckoned on San Francisco prices being so high. I noticed that Fred looked concerned, guessing that he might be on the border of losing a large weekly contract.

"Fine. Let's do a deal," he sighed.

I remembered how Rick had always told me that everything in life is negotiable. I stared back at Fred and then shook his hand in agreement.

He took out his notebook and scribbled another calculation. Then wrote a new figure on the paper.

"I'll look after your staff for $200 a week." He crossed his arms. "Now, how does that sound?"

"It's a deal."

Wow! Look at you girl--you just made your first big business negotiation!

My self-congratulatory feelings soon faded as I realised that Fred wasn't quite finished. "So how about dinner tonight?" he said. "You know, to solidify the deal."

Yuck! Why do men have to go and ruin a good thing?

"Let me check in with my husband and find out what he thinks about that." I chirped as I left the building.

Fred's face fell.

Sharp as a tack today, Willow.

Once inside the property, I inhaled the unmistakable odour of fresh paint. The walls were painted in a clinical white and the carpenters had been in to build a set of six workstations, placed in a 2 by 2 format. At the front of the boutique lay a small meeting area with a selection of colourful bordello chairs adorned with velvet bolsters. On the walls, there was a series of gold antiquated empty picture frames. I wasn't quite sure if they were meant to be like that or if the decorator hadn't quite gotten around to putting pictures inside. On each work table, there was a vintage airplane mounted on a stand. Each workstation had an airline cart on wheels positioned at the side of the unit. These carts were filled to the brim with makeup utensils and supplies, all branded with the unmistakable Plane Jane Beauty logo--a 1950s aircraft in the background shadowing a pop-art image of a beautiful flight attendant.

The whole vibe was decadent and original, and, as far as I could tell, unique.

I couldn't believe how well the mood board images had been transplanted into this vintage-inspired beauty salon. I knew instantly that the branding would be a hit. Mrs. G. had done a fabulous job, and in such a short time too. On closer examination, I noticed that the reception was an airline-style check-in. The designer had produced a batch of Plane Jane boarding cards to be given out to each client when they checked in for their appointments. At the rear of the store was a streamlined galley kitchen fitted out with stainless steel appliances. The area was cordoned off by a curtain just like you would see in an aircraft, except the curtain was designed with the unmistakable Plane Jane logo.

She's thought of every last detail!

But Mrs. G. wasn't quite finished. At the very back of the shop adjacent to the airline-styled bathroom, stood a 'Baggage Reclaim' area where guests could store their belongings and collect them before departing the store.

I checked the stowaway carts and made sure they had enough of the Plane Jane Beauty supplies for the interviewees to perform their makeovers.

Perfect! Everything is just so perfect!

Each bar cart contained bottles of cleanser, toner, three different types of moisturiser suited to different skin types, makeup brushes, and a selection of Plane Jane Beauty makeup items: lipstick in various shades, waterproof mascara, and regular mascara, a selection of eye shadows blush and bronzers and a complete collection of liquid foundations in every shade imaginable.

At 10:00 am as expected, the candidates began to show up at the door. I took the opportunity to sit at the 'check-in desk' and introduce myself to each one. First up was Carmen Monaco--a pretty redhead from Marin County. She was 30 years old and had years of experience in the industry. I checked my notes and saw that I had earmarked her for the manager role.

"Take a seat and familiarise yourself with the brand." I motioned to one of the workstations.

One by one, the other candidates appeared: Josefina Estepona--a charismatic girl in her mid-20s who hailed from Guatemala--and Jesse Shoreditch--the youngest candidate at only 18 years old and who had turned up after traveling overnight from Kansas. She possessed an ethereal-like beauty complete with high cheekbones, painted rosebud lips, and sparkling green eyes. She wore her long blonde hair high in a bun and oozed an air of *joie de vivre*. After checking over her CV, I knew that with the correct practical training she would be a sure-fire success but I also felt a sense of reluctance, due to her age.

Does she have the smarts to succeed?--the makeup artistry world could be cut-throat at the best of times.

Once everyone had turned up and checked in, I started the interview with a practical makeover.

"Thank you all for coming here today. Plane Jane Beauty is a brand-new company and, if successful today, you will be working in this flagship West Coast boutique."

The interviewees turned and smiled at each other.

"I want you to pair up and do a makeover on each other," I instructed. "You will find everything you need in the bar carts. You have 30 minutes each to perform a full makeover including a cleanse, tone, and moisturise. The theme of the day will be "Flight Attendant." I clapped my hands in true Mrs. G. style. "Now go to work."

I saw that Carmen took Jesse under her wing. I guessed she knew that working on such a beautiful face would make the most impact. Josefina paired up with a tall, young man in his early 20s. His name was Finn, and he had arrived from the local hairdressing and makeup artistry academy. I hoped he would be a success in the interview.

The next two candidates were both in their mid-20s: Luella Barclay from London and Serena Davenport from Connecticut.

As time strode on, I photographed each of the makeovers to better assist me in the hiring process. Once the 30 minutes were up, each couple changed places and did their makeovers.

After everyone had been photographed, I told the group to go to Fred's coffee bar next door and order coffee and snacks on the company tab. I needed to interview each candidate individually before making my final decision.

Finally, at 3:00 pm, I selected my team. I went into the café and joined my little group of prospective Plane Jane makeup artists.

A sea of hopeful faces sat in front of me and I didn't relish having to turn down two of the candidates, but based on the practicals and the individual interviews, my choices had been made.

"Well, first of all, I want to thank you all for coming today. The standard has been very high and you've all done a wonderful job." I scanned their faces as I spoke, dreading the next part. "If I call your name, would you please go back into the boutique and wait for me."

Silence descended over the room as I prepared to make the roll call of successful applicants. I looked up my list.

"Carmen Monaco." I smiled at Carmen as she hurried out of her chair, grabbing her belongings as she went.

"Josefina Estepona." I looked at Josefina, imagining how her raven black hair would look tied up in a ballet bun. Josefina looked confused. I could tell she didn't know whether she had been placed in the successful group or the unsuccessful group.

"Finn Finlayson." Finn smiled at me. I guessed that he was sure he had been successful.

I looked at the three remaining candidates: Jesse, Serena, and Luella. I knew whom I was taking on and I knew why I was hiring her. She may not be the most obvious candidate but I needed the youthful exuberance of a young person in the boutique. There was nothing technically wrong with either Serena's or Luella's makeovers but I suspected they had not been as enthusiastic as the other candidates.

"Jesse. Would you join the group please?" My stomach clenched as the other two girls stared at me, then at each other. I saw Jesse practically run for the door as the penny finally dropped with the two ladies.

"What the fuck?" shouted Luella as she grabbed her belongings. "You make us go through all that, then choose *her*?"

I stood my ground. "I'm not willing to discuss my hiring decisions but I want to thank you for your time today." I noticed Serena--the other candidate--starting to open her mouth too.

"You call yourself a fucking manager . . . what kind of shit show is this?" she said.

Serena, emboldened by Luella, decided to join in. "That one could hardly hold a makeup brush. " She pointed in the direction of Jesse. "What's your game? You haven't a clue how to hire!"

Bloody hell. They're not going down without a fight. This is not what I thought it would be.

A hush descended over the café as Fred appeared at my side.

"I'd like you two to leave my premises right now!" he ordered.

Both Serena and Luella scowled at me as they made to leave. They gathered up their belongings as Luella linked arms with Serena. Together, they intimidated me but I refused to let them know that.

I turned to Fred. "Thanks for that."

"Not a problem." He waved a hand. "If you get into any more trouble, just call me. I'll sort them out." Fred's face took on a serious expression.

"Well," I clasped my hands, "hopefully everything will be plain sailing from here on in, but thanks for the offer." I made a mental note to send out letters of rejection in the future.

Back in the pop-up store, I applauded my new team.

"Well done everyone and welcome to the Plane Jane Beauty Crew!"

The group hollered and laughed as the news finally sunk in--that they were the successful candidates. I noticed they had all been looking at Jesse and wondering which way it was going to go.

"I knew it! I just knew it!" said Finn as he shook my hand.

I gave a slight nod then sat down at the check-in area and called each candidate over one by one.

"Carmen, I'd like to hire you as the Boutique Manager." I handed her a white envelope containing her contract.

"Oh my God! Thank you." Her face flushed with excitement.

The memory of the earlier commotion in the café faded as I knew I had made the right decision hiring Carmen.

"Now go to the storeroom at the back of the shop and pick out your uniform. You'll need two dresses, a jacket, two white shirts, a pencil skirt, and a necktie."

"So we are going to dress up as flight attendants?" she said and skipped off. "I always wanted to be one of them when I was younger."

Laughing, I called out, "Josefina, can you come over please?" Josefina stepped over and stood in front of me. "You are going to be my second-in-command." I beamed. I recognised that she had never held a position with this kind of responsibility.

"You mean you want me to be the Assistant Manager?" she gushed with excitement as her face lit up. She wore 1960s-styled winged eyeliner and false eyelashes with a striking matte red lip.

I nodded. "You'll be expected to work closely with Carmen and take over from her when she's not here," I said, showing her a roster that I had printed out. "You'll also be expected to help train the other team members."

I knew this was a real step up for Josefina because, like myself, she had never stepped out from behind the makeup counter.

"You believe in me?" she asked, wide-eyed. Her hands crossed over her heart.

"I do," I said, smiling.

Josefina took her envelope and made her way to the back of the shop. We could hear the muffled screams as she celebrated with Carmen.

"Finn. You'll be the lead Makeup Artist." I handed him the envelope. I knew he was the most technically skilled out of the group. Finn smiled. "Thanks, Mrs. Campbell-Delgado."

"Go to the back of the store and collect your uniform. You'll need two jackets, two pairs of trousers, two white shirts, a tie and a pair of aviators. I want you to wear the glasses en route to work. Got that?"

Finn nodded, flashing his dimples. He looked good in the clothes he was wearing. I could only imagine the effect he would have on the clients when dressed in his fake pilot's uniform.

As Finn sauntered towards the back of the store to collect his uniform, I could tell that Jesse was almost bursting with excitement. I had left her until the end on purpose so that I could spend more time with her.

"Now, Jesse." I handed her the envelope. "This contract is for a trainee position. You'll be expected to shadow the more experienced members of the team and you'll fly to New York for further training with me when all the stores are up and running."

"New York!" she shouted. "I've never been to New York. I've never even been out of Kansas! Well, not until today." she beamed.

"Well, I appreciate your ambition and willingness to travel on a bus for two days to get here and I'm sure you'll do well. I want you to partner with Carmen. I'll make sure she takes you under her wing and looks after you. Do you have somewhere to stay?"

Jesse became downcast as the enormity of the move to San Francisco hit home.

"Um . . . not yet." She looked at her feet. "But I'll find somewhere." Her eyes took on a doleful look as she realised that finding anything affordable in the city would be a challenge.

My phone rang. It was Mrs. G.

"Willow! There's been a change of plans!" she crowed through the receiver. "I want you to launch the store tomorrow."

The colour drained from my face.

"But Mrs. Gerson . . ." I stuttered. "I just finished the recruitment session and I'm handing out the offer letters as we speak, the team hasn't been trained yet and I don't even know if there's enough stock in store for a soft launch. I--"

"I sent out the invitations to the important dignitaries and influencers and the local press will be attending." My boss talked over me.

"But, but--" I started to protest.

"Do you need me to find another COO, Willow?"

"No!" I shouted, "I can manage!"

There was no point in arguing. If Mrs. G. said there was going to be a soft opening, then that's what would happen. End of bloody story!

I turned to face Jesse.

"We open tomorrow." I shrugged. "So, you're not going back to Kansas tonight."

Jesse picked up on my serious tone. Mrs. G. had just left me with one helluva problem and I needed all hands on deck.

I stared at her. "The only problem now is your accommodation." I tapped my lips with the pen, then got down to business. "Call your mum and tell her we'll put you up in a hotel for the first week and then you'll have to find somewhere else to stay."

Jesse squealed. "Yes, let me call her! Oh my God! I can't believe this!"

I began to have doubts about choosing Jesse over one of the older, more experienced candidates, but then I remembered the attitude of both Luella and Serena and re-affirmed to myself that I had made the right decision. I just had to make the plan work.

"Let me check my hotel and see if they have rooms available. Now you go and choose your uniform with the others." I ordered, desperate for a moment alone to gather my thoughts.

I felt like Mrs. G. was sabotaging my efforts, especially when the candidates had only just been hired.

Why on earth does she want me to open the store tomorrow? That is way too soon.

But when I thought about it, I guessed it must be a financial decision. I understood she needed to gain a return on her investment as soon as possible. I remembered the card she gave me and decided now was the perfect time to make contact with George. I took out my phone and texted him.

Hi George!

'Willow here. I'm in San Francisco and I just heard the news that we open tomorrow! I'm panic-stricken. I'm so not ready to do this George. What shall I do?'

I placed the phone on the table and took a sip of the coffee. George got back to me straight away.

'Wills!'

'I wondered how long it would take you to contact me! Now. You've not to worry about a thing. I'm here in the background orchestrating the whole show. Just do what you need to do to get through and leave the rest to me.'

I exhaled a sigh of relief. I wasn't alone after all.

'Thank you, George.'

***

Later that afternoon, satisfied that Jesse was safe and sound and settled in her room--she was located two doors away from me--I left her. "OK then," I knocked on the door frame as I left, "I'll swing by at 8:30." I made my way to leave. "We'll walk to Fred's for breakfast, OK?"

"Yes Ma'am!" Jesse hugged me before grabbing her phone to call her mum again.

Back in my room and relieved that the day was over, I kicked off my airline-edition shoes and threw my coat over the suitcase. Then, as Jesse did a few minutes ago, I threw myself on top of the freshly made-up bed and breathed a huge sigh of relief.

I lay back and closed my eyes. *I did it.* I had done what Mrs. G. asked me to do. I allowed myself to feel secretly pleased but, as usual, that only lasted a few moments. Jake had been texting me all afternoon. Then I realised that Mrs. G. had inadvertently given me the perfect excuse not to fly to Ireland.

I lay on the soft duvet, planning in my head how to word my final text message to him when my eyes wandered to a small bunch of pink peonies wrapped in cellophane lying on the desk next to the phone.

What the . . . ? Did Mrs. G. send me flowers? No, she wouldn't. That's not her style.

I got up from the bed and picked up the envelope, scrambling to open it as quickly as possible. Inside lay a small white card with the words, **Meet me at the Golden Gate Bridge, tonight at 8:00 pm. Love, Rick**.

"What the hell's he playing at?" I mumbled.

I threw the card onto the bed and stared at it like it was infected with some virulent virus. Worse still. I knew I would go.

CHAPTER FIVE

Golden Gate Revelations

The cab driver dropped me off at the entrance to the bridge. I was only 15 minutes late, but there was no sign of Rick.

The driver gave me a quizzical look. "Just here?"

"This will do, thanks," I responded trying to look like I knew what I was doing, although I had questioned my every move since reading that damn card. But, as usual, curiosity had gotten the better of me.

I watched as the taxi sped off. Night had descended fast, and traffic on the bridge appeared to be relentless. A few others were hanging around. I checked my phone-8:25 pm. *Where the hell is he? He better not stand me up!*

At 8:30, as I was about to pack up my shame and embarrassment and hail the next empty cab that came my way, a sleek black car sped to a halt just in front of me. Rick jumped out.

"So sorry, darling! My meeting went on longer than it should, and then we got stuck in traffic." Eyeing me up and down, he smiled approvingly. "Very nice. Never seen you in a pink dress before.

I blushed. *Why did he always have this pull on me?*

"What's up?" I asked, trying to regain my composure.

"Nothing. I just wanted to show you the bridge at night--it's the most romantic place, Willow." He smiled as he pulled out a large white daisy from his jacket pocket. "Now the rule is if you are gonna walk the bridge with me, you must wear this flower and put it behind your ear."

I looked at him in surprise, "Are you off your rocker?"

Rick looked confused. "Oh, come on." He scoffed. "You must know the song! It's like the city's theme."

"Nope!"

"It's a famous song!"

"Sorry." I shook my head. "I have no clue what you are talking about."

"Hold on." He pulled out his phone and clicked on the YouTube app. The song was already lined up. "Listen," he said as Scott McKenzie sang the first few beats of "San Francisco." I didn't get it, not until I listened to the lyrics.

"*If you're going to San Francisco be sure to wear some flowers in your hair,*" Rick repeated the line. He smiled at me, eyes glinting under the moonlight, and put his arms in mine.

I flinched.

"I'm allowed to do this Willow," he said. "We're not quite divorced yet." I turned and faced him.

"What is it?" he looked perplexed.

"I don't know what your game is here--inviting me to this bridge at night, acting like we're a couple of love birds!" I pulled my arm away from him. "And let's put this small act of *ownership* to bed, shall we?"

Rick tutted and shook his head.

"Aww . . . lighten up for Chrissakes."

"You don't own me Rick and you have no rights whatsoever to my body, got it?"

Rick stared at his feet.

"And as for that carry-on in the closet earlier, that is so not on."

"O.K." Rick held up his hands and took two steps back from me, "Message received. Loud and clear."

To passersby, I'm sure we looked like a regular couple arguing on the bridge. Memories of our first meeting in Devonshire's came rushing back. I recalled how it had been an instant attraction as I had stood behind my makeup counter-his confidence, his swagger, his American accent . . . what woman in my position could resist his charm?

And my life before meeting Rick had been, shall we say, stagnant. I had grown bored; bored with doing the same work, bored with having the same conversations . . . Yeah, what woman in my situation could resist a Rick walking into her life?

I mean, really?

Rick bowed his head and pulled his collar up tighter. I felt a chill in the air on this Californian evening.

"So how are things with you and your *baby mama*, Bella?"

I thought about the damage that Isabella de la Souza had done to our marriage. How determined she had been to split us up, calling the authorities on us, accusing us of having a 'green card marriage' and then proclaiming to be carrying Rick's child.

He appeared agitated. "I finally got her to do a DNA test."

"You did?" I was shocked, and dreading the answer, "So how did that go down?"

Rick stopped walking and turned and stared at me. He looked sad. "The baby wasn't mine." His shoulders sagged in defeat.

That fucking bitch!

"I'm sorry, Rick." A tsunami of emotion cascaded over me. "That must be hard to bear."

I took a step back as I took in the news.

He had always insisted the baby wasn't his . . .

Her lies. Her damn lies. Things could have turned out so differently if it hadn't been for Isabella.

Rick remained silent.

"Is this the real reason why you wanted to walk the bridge tonight?"

More silence. I noticed a solitary tear navigate its way down his cheek. I stopped walking and threw my arms around him. My head was spinning as I attempted to think of things to say to console him.

"She's dead to me," Rick whispered. The moon glistened as the waves below us started to whip up. I was chilled to the bone standing in my flimsy pink dress and thin coat. My kitten heels pinching my toes. Rick must have sensed my discomfort.

"Shall we turn back?" he asked.

"Yeah," I hugged myself. "I think we should--I need a hot chocolate to warm me up."

Rick stopped in his tracks. "Can I get another hug?"

"Of course, you can." The familiar scent of his cologne infiltrated my nostrils as I sensed him release a sob. I stroked the back of his head, not sure what else I could do to comfort him.

He looked up at me. "I fucked up, Willow. I didn't realise how good I had it with you . . ."

"Stop it, Rick!" Now, I was in charge. "Look at me." I stared at him forcing him to look back at me. "Everything's going to work out fine," I said firmly. "You'll meet someone else."

I put my finger under his chin and lifted his head. I didn't recognize my own voice.

Who is this person talking?

Rick's face took on a childlike expression, "You mean there's no chance we . . . ?"

I shook my head gently and let the question linger. I didn't need to say anything. Rick continued sniffing and nodding his head before breaking into a sob.

"I'm sorry," he held up one hand and covered his face with the other. "Sorry," he said again.

"Hey," I pulled on his hand covering his face, "Hey," I said softly. "You and I." I took in a deep breath, "You and I--we were a mistake. A glorious mistake. I'll always be grateful to you for stealing me away and making my life so much more--how shall I say--*interesting*?" I sighed a little, "But you know as well as I do that it would be an even bigger mistake to get back together."

"You think so?" Rick looked defeated.

I nodded and put my arm in his and steered him back the way we came. "Now, c'mon and buy me that hot chocolate. I'm bloody freezing."

***

Twenty minutes later we were back in the city, traipsing up and down Lombard Street, looking for a suitable place to get a hot chocolate. Neither of us knew the city well enough to be familiar with the best eateries and wine bars until I stumbled on the bar I had been in earlier on my first day in the city.

"Let's go in here," I said, pulling Rick by the arm. He didn't look too impressed. It wasn't the usual wine bar he liked to frequent in New York City--this was way more rustic chic for his sophisticated tastes.

"Why do you want to go in here?" he whined.

"They serve their chocolate Martinis with real Ghirardelli chocolate! And I know the bartender." I winked.

"Should have known." A wry smile shot across his face. "Can't take you anywhere."

"He's not very nice, dresses way too young for his age, and is rather rude." I attempted to explain but Rick had lost interest. I caught him eyeing up a pretty blonde. *Waste of time speaking to him.*

I strode up and perched on a bar stool and waited till there was a break in the crowd before catching the bartender's eye. Rick had disappeared into the crowd, leaving me alone.

"Well . . . well. Look who it is." The bartender smirked crossing his arms. "So, what brings you back here?" He gave me a half-smile. "Wait a minute . . . didn't you say you were never coming back?"

"What kind of welcome is that?" I replied, stiffening in my seat, wishing that Rick would hurry up and extract himself from the conversation with the blonde. "Do you treat all your customers so rudely?"

"Nope!" He chirped. "Only the ones that deserve it."

"So, now that you find it impossible to stay away . . . what can I get you?" He tapped his fingers on the bar as he waited on my response. A lock of his hair fell in front of one eye.

I looked around for Rick, caught his eyes, and indicated for him to hurry up and join me.

"Um . . . two hot chocolates please."

"Two?" Pat looked surprised. "Hot chocolates?"

"Yes. That's what I said. Two hot chocolates please." I made my sentence long and drawn out for added effect with emphasis on the word, 'please.'

"Look, lady . . . this is a bar. Any liquor in these hot chocolates?"

Rick turned up and sat down on the bar stool beside me.

"Make mine a whiskey, pal."

"And you?" he stared at me.

Rick nodded. "She'll take a shot of whiskey in hers."

Appalled that he was making decisions for me, I nudged him in the elbow to shush him up. "No. I'll have a shot of Drambuie in mine please." I smiled at the barman.

He gave me a half-smile then turned his back to prepare the drinks.

"Who was that you were chatting up?" I asked, turning my attention back to Rick.

"Oh, she's aaah . . ." Rick looked uncomfortable. "I'm, uh . . . meeting up with her later."

"Wow," I raised my brows and shook my head in amazement. "You're a quick worker, I'll give you that," I stated my mood darkening.

Now that I had seen Rick in action with another female, I understood that I had just been another conquest for him. I was relieved I had moved on.

The bartender returned with our drinks. He wore a surly expression.

"So. Are you enjoying your stay in our dear city?" he asked, all attention on me as Rick checked his phone.

"Yes," I said. "But," I paused, "I haven't had time to explore yet . . .

I've been recruiting for a beauty pop-up store."

"Well, congratulations! Just what this city needs--another nail bar." Patrick threw his tea towel over his shoulder and turned to walk away. The mocking tone of his voice irritated me.

"It's not a nail bar. It's a full-service makeup salon. You should come in sometime and have some work done." I added. I couldn't help but smile at my own wit.

Nice one, Willow. Sharp.

"Aw . . . we've got a funny one here, have we?" Patrick raised an eyebrow and winked at me, his attitude appearing to thaw a little.

Rick butted in. "Hi. Rick Delgado." He held his hand out to Patrick. "Here on business and bumped into my lovely *wife!*" He put his arm around me and squeezed me tight.

I wiggled out of Rick's grasp, mortified that he had called me his wife.

"About to be *ex*-wife!" I interjected, feeling deeply uncomfortable with Rick's interlude.

"I'm a lucky man." Rick laughed and raised his glass to Patrick.

"You are, indeed." Patrick mocked as he turned away to serve other customers.

What does he mean by that? I wondered. I couldn't quite grasp whether he was being serious or sarcastic.

Rick and I sat on for another half hour, laughing and joking about our whirlwind relationship.

"There's something I always wanted to ask you," I said.

"What's that?"

"Why me?" I asked. "Of all the girls that worked in Devonshire's? All of them were gorgeous--way prettier than me--so why me?"

Rick sat back in on his bar stool, the small of his back supported by a piece of carved driftwood.

He mulled over my question. "Something to do with reading a book, I suppose. You were different. You got my attention." He was staring at me. I sensed the bartender glance at both of us out of the corner of my eye.

"Was that it? A bloody book?!" A wave of disappointment washed over me.

"You were cute too," Rick added quickly. "And anyway, you were supposed to have been working, not reading a book behind your makeup counter! I guess that got my attention."

Patrick interrupted before I could reply.

"Would you like another round?"

Rick shook his head, stood up, and made to leave. "Got to get this girl home." I caught him winking at him like he was talking some kind of boy code. Something about that gesture made me want to explain to the barman that I wasn't his girl but there was no time to explain. Rick planted a bunch of dollar bills on the bar and held out my coat. I took it from him and marched out of the bar. I was mortified and annoyed at Rick but a recurring thought left me ill at ease--*Why do I care so much about what that bloody cheeky barman thinks of me?*

I shrugged off the thought and waited on the pavement till Rick caught up with me.

"Bartender's got the hots for you!" he said.

"What? Don't be so daft!" I kicked a pebble as I mulled over his words.

"You know he puts too much ice in his drinks." Rick's tone was defiant.

"Yeah, well . . . ," I agreed.

"Too much ice waters the drink down. This means he doesn't have to put much liquor in. I'm not even a little bit tipsy, are you?"

"I am." My head was swimming.

"You're such a lightweight," Rick grinned. "And that guy's cheap."

"OK, OK, that's quite enough, Rick."

"What? You like him? You like the cheapo bartender?"

"Just stop. Will you? And no. I don't like him. After you and Jake, I'm off men. Forever!"

Rick walked me toward the entrance to the hotel. He stood at the doorway of the building and made no attempt to come up to my room. He had finally gotten the message and I'm guessing his thoughts were already on the blonde he had met in the bar.

"I'm flying back to New York tomorrow morning," he said.

"Oh?"

"Yep. A good trip, I would say." He winked. "Business deals were a success and I got to meet up with you." He put his hand in his jacket pocket and pulled out a little gift-wrapped box. "I wanted to give you this."

He placed the box in my hand and closed my fingers over it. My eyes narrowed as I held the box. It was small and light, it reminded me a lot of a ring box.

Please, don't propose again. Please.

"Don't look too worried." Rick patted my shoulder. "It's just my wedding ring. Thought you could melt it down and use it for cash."

I didn't know whether to laugh or cry.

"Call me when you arrive back in New York, and we can discuss the divorce arrangements." Then he kissed me on the side of the cheek and walked off, never turning back.

CHAPTER SIX

Rat Pack

I awoke at 7:00 am with the sunshine streaming in through the gaps in my window blinds.

I threw the covers back and exhaled. "Today's the day!"

The room was untidy from the night before and I managed to rustle up a pair of leggings and a baggy jumper from the depths of my trolley bag. I pulled my hair back into a tiny ponytail and pulled on my runners. The plan was to nip out and go for a quick walk before the day was consumed with the grand store opening.

Once outside in the morning sunshine, I strolled along Lombard Street once more and looked for a café where I could buy a strong cup of coffee. Harvey's Diner was open and already getting a lot of business.

This will do perfectly.

After purchasing my cup of coffee, I turned around and bumped straight into Patrick. The bartender from Brodie's. He was walking a small black dog on a leash.

"Well . . . look who it is." He smiled. It felt strangely weird to see him in the full light of day instead of the dimmed bar lighting in Brodie's. "You're up early."

I felt a little unnerved. "Big day today." I beamed.

"And who's this little guy?" I asked stooping down to clap the little black dog.

"*Her* name is Lola."

"Oh. I see." *How the hell was I supposed to know the dog was a girl?*

"She's our rescue dog." He smiled back, looking down at his beloved Lola. The dog looked up at him, her tongue hanging out one side of her mouth.

"She's a bit of a princess but we love her," He smiled, turning his attention back to me. "I never did get to find out your name."

I held my hand out to shake his. "My name's Willow. And you?"

"Patrick Brodie . . . although everyone calls me Pat or sometimes I get Paddy." He appeared a little self-conscious in the broad light of day. "But you can call me Pat."

"Um . . . no thanks."

Pat looked confused.

"It's just I prefer to call people by their proper names." I smiled up at him.

"Whatever." He shrugged, then pulled his dog on the leash. "So, I guess I'll see you in the bar later?"

"Um . . . you might! Depends on how the day goes."

I felt like an idiot talking to him. I felt incapable of drumming up a decent intellectual conversation.

"Well, good luck today, Willow. I'm sure the launch will be a huge success." Pat wore a slightly confused look on his face like he was struggling to think of something to say.

Then he was off, walking his Lola up Lombard Street while I watched on.

There's just something about a man walking a dog.

***

Back in the shop, I looked at my phone--it was 9:50 am, just ten minutes before the grand opening of Plane Jane Beauty and already people were queuing up along the pavement. I switched on my phone and saw 56 text messages from Mrs. G.

The relentless pinging of notifications on my phone was driving me crazy but I could tell the marketing campaign orchestrated from New

York was building a frenzy of interest here in San Francisco.

The phone pinged once more.

Wills!

Are you all set for the launch? Text me if you need anything. Here for you as always.

George.

I exhaled a sigh of relief. It felt great to have this unknown person on my side. George's text messages were slowly becoming something I looked forward to receiving when I switched on my phone.

I wonder what he looks like. Bet he's a happily married family man with a dog and kids. I smiled at the thought.

My crew members were all applying last-minute touches to their makeup at their workstations while I tried to go through my checklist before opening.

I thought the team looked fantastic in their 1950s styled uniforms and noticed that Josefina had hitched her skirt up so that it looked like a miniskirt.

"Josefina, that skirt needs to be at knee level."

Josefina looked a tad embarrassed but pulled the skirt down to a more appropriate length. I could hear her mutter something under her breath but decided to let it go. It wasn't a good time to be chastising new employees. I was hellbent on fostering good relationships and needed my team onside.

I gathered the gang around me for a pep talk, just like Mrs. G. used to do on the shop floor at D'Arcy's.

"Everyone--gather around."

Carmen, Jesse, Josefina, and Finn stood beside me.

"You all look fabulous!" I beamed, scanning the group. "Now, the press will be arriving shortly." I looked over at Carmen. "You are in charge of looking after them. Make sure they get a gift bag to take home."

"Will do!" said Carmen.

As the most experienced member of my team, I felt confident leaving her with the most important tasks. My mind flitted back to that fateful afternoon in D'Arcy's when Mrs. G had informed Jackson and I that we would be looking after the press at our new counter in store. It had been a disaster.

I shook the memory away. Nerves were starting to kick in. There was so much riding on this store being a success. I looked over and saw Jesse staring at her feet. I knew she was out of her depth. She was going to need some direction to build her confidence.

"Josefina--take Jesse and man the doors, make sure everyone gets a glass of fizz as they enter," I ordered. "And don't forget to offer non-alcoholic drinks as an option!"

Josefina saluted me and rushed over to Jesse.

"Finn, you're on check-in duty." I read from my to-do list. "Make sure everyone gets a promo card offering 25% off today's purchase."

Finn nodded. He was fairly quiet and stoic--a real benefit to the team, I anticipated that he was someone who could take control when things got out of hand.

I gently placed my hands on the shoulders of Jesse and Josefina. "Now remember the store motto--"In-flight Beauty On Demand--We're in it for the long haul." Please be kind to everyone you meet, no matter how trying they might be." I smiled. I handed each team member a white card with a number inscribed on it.

"These are your targets for today."

The crew each took a card and stared at it.

"You hit your target and then help another team member who might be struggling, OK?"

The girls nodded in agreement but Finn looked perplexed.

"But doesn't that go against the grain?" He pushed his glasses onto the top of his head. "I mean what's the point of hitting your own target just to go and help someone else out?"

"It's called teamwork!" I threw up my arms and smiled. "We all have a store target to meet. We hit the store target, then we all benefit."

It was a light bulb moment for Finn. I guessed he had never had the opportunity to work that way before with his limited experience.

"We are a small team, and we need to stick together, got it?" I looked around the beauty parlour.

"Got it!" They replied in unison.

I checked my watch. It was 09:59 am.

"OK, let's get this show on the road." I clapped. "Jesse, open the doors!"

The throng of excited shoppers burst into the store, creating an electric atmosphere in the boutique. The press team arrived at the same time as the customers, catching us all off guard. But the crew sprang into action, offering prospective customers plastic champagne flutes filled with bubbly, hand massages, and spritzes of L'Eau de Sky--the Plane Jane fragrance--while a select few enjoyed sit-down makeovers at the workstations.

I looked on as the newspaper photographer took photos of the store activity, while the reporter--a young woman in her early 20s--tried her best to interview me amidst the melee.

Finn was positioned by the cash register at the check-in station, expertly ringing up sales, wrapping purchases and capturing customer details on the computer system, using his charisma to charm the customers.

I felt proud and made it my mission to let the reporter know about it. Josefina had showered her with free samples of the night cream while Jesse worked the Shea butter hand cream into her hands.

"So, why the airline theme for this new beauty parlour? I mean what's the thought processes behind the brand?" The reporter asked, enjoying the lavish attention.

I swung into full PR mode.

"The proprietor of the brand, Mrs. Gigi Gerson, former owner of D'Arcy's Department Store in Queens, New York, was a flight attendant in her younger days," I stated as the reporter recorded my voice into her phone. "She was always very strict with her staff at D'Arcy's and I'm guessing this was because of her airline background. Anyway, she was insistent that the team members--or should I say *crew* members--dressed in the style of flight attendants." I looked around the store. "They all look fabulous--don't they?"

"Yes." The reporter's eyes followed mine. "I see what you mean. They all look terribly smart."

I could tell I was winning her over.

"But you are only going to open for six months? Is that correct? And would that not be to the detriment of the San Francisco retail community? I mean you just flitted in from New York City. You intend to open up here for six months, then you pack up and leave again?" she shook the pen as she spoke, distracting me.

Shit! I hoped she wouldn't ask that question.

How would George respond to this question?

I clasped my hands behind my back and took up some floor space. I had witnessed Mrs. G. adopt this stance during difficult days in the store.

Just breathe, Willow. Take your time. Don't let her intimidate you. Think of Alicia Keys singing 'Empire State of Mind'--would she take this shit? No, I don't think so.

"Yes. That's correct. We have taken out a six-month lease, but we're not a 'fly by night operation--sorry no pun intended." I gave her my best condescending smile. " If the store is a success then, of course, we will take out a longer lease., I remembered the store motto. "We're in it for the long haul"

Where the hell did all of that come from?

The reporter stared at me, looking pensive but soon appeared satisfied with the explanation. I decided enough was enough. I had to get on with looking after the guests.

"Would you excuse me? I must re-fill those shelves with more stock." I smiled and nodded as I stepped away.

"Yes." She smiled back. "Go ahead. I think I have everything I need." She put her phone away in her jacket pocket.

"Thanks. If you need any more information give me a call...do you have my number?" I asked, scanning the boutique which was getting busier by the minute. I turned and bumped into Patrick, instantly forgetting about my conversation with the reporter.

"Oh! Sorry." I looked him up and down.

Patrick stared at me. "Hey Willow! I'm looking for Carmen. Have you seen her?" He looked over the top of my head. I followed his gaze toward the back of the store.

"Carmen? She's in the back, filling up champagne glasses," I said.

How is he connected to Carmen? I wondered, watching as he made his way towards the 'Baggage Reclaim' area. He looked different out from behind his bar--wearing a crew neck pale blue jumper and a pair of faded chinos. I could tell he had put a spot of gel in his hair as it didn't fall forward into his face the way it did when he was at work. Today, he looked well turned out.

Jeez, Willow, get a grip!

I gave him the once over. I looked on with interest as he greeted Carmen with a big hug. I could tell they were very familiar with each other.

Funny, I would never put Carmen down as his type.

She was small, dainty, and very glam, in a 1950s pinup girl kind of way.

She was chatting to him as she poured the champagne, all business-like in her flight attendant uniform with her red hair tied up in a bun. I could tell they liked each other. I looked away.

Just then I heard a scream.

"Oh my God! There's a rat!"

What the . . . ?

I shuddered as I scanned the shop floor.

The store flew into an uproar as customers stood on the airline-styled chairs and shrieked while others ran into the staff room closing the door behind them. The remainder of the customers ran out of the shop, screaming as they went. Platters of cheese cubes lay sprawled across the shop floor as three black rats munched away.

"No!" I screamed inside. "This can't be happening! Not at my store opening!"

I had no choice but to ask the last remaining group of staff and customers to vacate the shop and lock the door behind me. When I was sure that everyone was out of the building, I gathered my crew together.

"Go to Fred's! I'll be back as soon as I can!"

Then I ran up the street towards the reporter. I grabbed her by the arm. "Please don't write about this . . ."

She yanked her arm from my grasp.

"I beg you!" I cried. "Please don't! My boss's business will be in ruins, and we'll all be out of a job."

She looked indignant. "But I have to!" she frowned. "I must report this." She looked irritated I even suggested she shouldn't.

I turned to the photographer. "What about you? Are you going to deliver those images?"

"Yep--already sent. Sorry," he shrugged, smacking the gum in his mouth.

A wave of fury built up inside me.

How could they be so cruel?

"Then give me those!" I took the gift bags from their hands and stomped back toward Fred's coffee bar.

This cannot be happening. This cannot!

"Look. I'm sorry," the reporter called back. "We all have jobs to do."

Fred's coffee bar had been inundated with my customers. I threw myself down in a booth. Defeated. Head in hands.

What am I going to tell Mrs G.?

"So, you found out about the rat problem?" Fred asked, staring down at me. He shifted his eyes from side to side, not quite able to hold my stare.

I slammed my hands on the Formica table. "You knew?" I narrowed my eyes. "And you didn't bother to tell me?" I screeched, enraged. "What's the matter with you?"

Fred took a bench opposite me. His expression is a mixture of emotions.

"What was I supposed to say?" he rubbed his palms together as if attempting to make fire.

"You could have hinted at least." I rolled my eyes.

"Look." He ran a hand through his greasy hair. "Why do you think the premises were vacant all this time? The whole street has a problem! Has for decades."

I scrunched my face in disgust. "Even you? But you serve food here!"

Fred shifted on the bench, lowering his voice as he spoke. "We've got everything under control. The 'rat guys' come in every week to check. We're safe."

Well, now I just lost my appetite.

I tossed a napkin on the table.

"Anyway, none of this is your fault, it's down to the person who took out the lease." Fred grinned, like that made this all better. "They should have done their due diligence," he said. "They should have checked stuff out." Fred waved his finger, back on track now.

He was right. Nothing else for it but to call Mrs. G. and tell her what happened.

"Willow." Carmen approached Patrick. Her arm wrapped around his back. "Pat is offering to give everyone a free drink at Brodie's Bar to make up for things."

"Oh, that's just bloody great! That's rich!" I stood up, face-to-face with him. "So you get the chance to sweep in and scoop up all my customers? Help yourself there, Patrick!"

Carmen interjected, "He's only trying to help, Mrs. Campbell-Delgado."

"It's Campbell," I snapped.

Carmen looked flustered. "Sorry. I didn't know. It says on the contract your surname is . . ."

"Look. That doesn't matter right now." I turned and stared at Patrick. "Take them. Take all my customers! I'm about to be the laughingstock of San Francisco in a few hours when the evening newspaper comes out."

Patrick held his phone in his hand. "It's out. Already. In fact, I think you've gone kinda viral by now."

"Give me that!" I grabbed the phone from his hand and felt crushed as Plane Jane Beauty's reputation went down the pan. Customers and beauty influencers had posted their videos and the news was everywhere.

"The Rat Pack Strikes Again!"

"San Francisco Beauty Launch Invaded By Rats!"

" Chocks Off & Rats Away At Plane Jane Beauty!"

I was horrified. Sick to my stomach. I looked on at Patrick trying to contain his laughter as another video of the fiasco appeared online.

"You're going to love this one." He held his free hand over his mouth. Then showed me the phone screen. Carmen glanced at it before me and elbowed him in the side.

"Rat Attack at Plane Jane Beauty Launch!"

I scowled as my phone rang. It was Mrs. G. *Just great. Her timing is impeccable.*

"'Scuse me. I have to take this call in private." I stalked off hearing Carmen whisper, "stop!" as I imagined Patrick was cracking up. Fred indicated for me to go behind the counter and sit in a private area away from the hustle and bustle of the café.

Twenty minutes later, I came off the phone. I got the impression that Mrs. G. knew she had messed up, but she was never going to admit that. Instead, she told me to close up the shop and arrange for an exterminator. Right about now, she was getting on the phone with the local newspaper to figure out damage control, but we both knew it was too late.

I looked over to see Carmen giggling with Patrick as they scanned their phones for further stories of our rat invasion.

Can this day get any worse?

"OK. Fred. I'm going back to my hotel to have a think." I looked over at Carmen and Patrick.

"I can't concentrate in here."

"Call me if you need company." he winked.

I scrunched up my face in disgust and walked out of the café. I gave a quick toss of my hair as I passed Patrick. He was laughing at something Carmen had said.

"Hey Willow!" I heard him call over the jingle of the bells on the door. "No doubt I'll see you in Brodie's later." He smiled as Carmen waved goodbye.

I looked at them.

No you bloody well will not!

Back in my hotel room, the phone rang off the hook while Mrs. G. scrambled to find new premises. Our store opening had been an out-and-out disaster and none of us wanted to go back to the infested premises, at least not while there was a gang of rats in residence.

At 7:30 pm the phone rang again, "Mrs. G." I sighed and picked up the phone, faking cheer.

"Willow, I found new premises! I want you to pick up the keys from Brodie's Bar tonight at 8:00 pm and then go and check out the premises on Lombard. If everything is suitable, we'll launch in a week."

She sounded excited. *What's she so excited about? Has she been drinking?* I frowned.

"But what about the press?" I grimaced.

"Too late for that, dear. The news already came out. It's everywhere!" she exclaimed. "Every. Where," she repeated. "Don't you have My Face or Twittergram?" she scolded. "I was in touch with my PR consultant, George, and he says we have to make the most of our name is in lights right now. The show must go on dear. We just have to roll with it." she said brightly.

"Right. Well." I didn't know what to say.

"Is there a problem, Willow?" Mrs. G.'s tone changed. I knew there was no point in arguing with her.

"Nope. Nothing I can't handle," I declared, rolling my eyes.

For a fleeting moment, I wished I was standing behind my makeup counter in Barneys, doing makeovers and going for regular tea breaks with the girls and that other normal workday stuff. Being a manager, and being in charge, was a whole different ballgame.

I downed the last dregs of my coffee, threw my coat on, and made my way out of the hotel towards Lombard Street.

Of all the bloody places it has to be this dump again! I peered in Brodie's and saw Patrick holding court behind the bar. He stopped serving, passed his customer over to the barmaid, and came out from behind the bar to greet me.

"We meet again." He stood in front of me with his arms folded across his chest. "So I guess you're after these?" He held a bunch of keys in his hand. I nodded, my dislike for him growing by the minute.

"You got over your little shock yet?" he asked, a look of concern on his face as a lock of sandy-blonde hair fell into his eye.

"Yes. I have actually."

He threw one arm into his canvas golf jacket and indicated for me to follow him. "Your boss called at just the right time."

"She did?"

"Not she, he! Some guy called George? Her PR guy?" He asked if I knew of vacant premises that would be suitable for a pop-up store." He opened the door to the staff car parking, "I figured he needed it for you guys."

"George? Did he call you? But why?"

He stood in front of me, both his hands in pockets, staring at me. "My family has a vacant space, that," he cupped a hand to his lips and whispered, "would make the perfect rat-free pop-up store for you." He grinned, dropping his hands.

His attitude really annoyed me.

"Glad to hear you're enjoying the situation so much. Must be great to glean your entertainment from other people's misfortune." I shifted my weight from foot to foot.

Patrick ignored me and climbed into the driver's seat of his shiny red Hilux wagon and invited me to climb into the passenger seat.

"Get in." He called through, reaching over to open the passenger door for me.

I regretted not changing out of my airline uniform. I hiked the skirt up and attempted to climb into the wagon as ladylike as I could. I noticed him glance at my legs. I caught his eye and drew him a dirty look. He turned away.

"What kind of music do you like?" he asked, fiddling with the radio, as a famous nursery rhyme screeched out of the speaker.

"Sorry 'bout that." He scrambled to clear away some empty paper bags and detritus from the local hamburger joint.

I pulled the seat belt over me and buckled myself in, pulling my skirt down as far over my knees as possible.

"I like all sorts. Have you got any Burt Bacharach? Dionne Warwick?"

"How old are you?" he laughed. "Is that kind of music not a bit passé for a hip chick like you?"

"Hip?" I scoffed. "Never been called that before!" I glanced at him as we sped off towards the freeway. I felt anxious now. "Where are we go-ing?"

He looked over at me as I clutched onto my bag that was sitting on my knees.

"Thought I'd steal you away and show you a bit of the city . . ." Patrick smiled. "Is that OK? When I get the chance I like to sneak away from the bar and go for a drive." He looked over at me. "These days it's the only time I seem to get to myself."

"Well . . . mm . . . you see, I'm a very busy lady, Patrick." I clucked. "It hasn't exactly been the best of days."

He tilted his head to the side as we pulled up at a red light. He appeared to soften. "No. I guess not. Hopefully, this will relax you."

He turned the radio station to the classical music channel.

The next minutes passed in silence. *Awkward.*

"Look." Patrick broke the silence. "If it helps any, I'm sorry for laugh-ing at your predicament."

"A bit late for that now, is it not?" I folded my arms across my chest and stared out of the window.

"Wasn't very adult of me . . . I . . . er . . . I should know better."

I drew him a look and remained silent.

"Are you hungry?"

I nodded. I was famished. I hadn't eaten for most of the day.

He pulled off the freeway at the nearest exit and swerved into a drive-thru burger joint.

"You got to try one of our famous 'Over and Out' burgers. The best burger joint on the west coast."

"If you insist."

After placing his order, he pulled into a parking space while we waited.

He drummed his fingers on his jean-clad knee, while I gripped my trusty Kate Spade. I noted my knuckles were white.

I guessed it was one of those situations where you could cut the tension with a knife.

"Tell me about Glasgow. What's it like?" he asked. "It's a place I always wanted to visit. Once had a pal who went to Glasgow University."

"Oh, well, Glasgow is a great place." I sighed thinking about my youth. *Oh those teenage years* I grinned. "Such a great place. We certainly like to party," I barked out a short laugh then cleared my throat. "But we also like to look after each other."

"Sounds like my kind of place." Patrick nodded. "So, why New York?" He looked out the window. "New York is a very difficult city if you don't have the right connections."

"Believe you are and you will be," I whispered and smiled to myself.

"Sorry?" Patrick shifted in his seat, taking the delivery through the vehicle window, I made a face and smacked my bag.

"It's my motto. 'Believe you are and you will be.' I took a chance."

Patrick handed me a coke and a burger. "And this chance," he glanced over, "was it the guy from last night?"

What's with all the personal questions?

I nodded.

I felt this questioning was becoming too personal for comfort, so I bit into the burger. "Oh my!" I exclaimed--it was every bit as delicious as Patrick had promised.

"Right?" Patrick took a bite of his own burger and sighed. "It's so good!" he said with his mouth full.

"Delicious." I licked my upper lip. "I see what you mean." I grappled with the drink and burger, spilling shredded lettuce onto my lap. He leaned down and scooped up some shreds of lettuce that had fallen onto the floor of the Hilux, placing it into the paper bag.

"So tell me about Brodie's Bar." I said, popping a fry into my mouth.

"Brodie is my last name. I own the bar--well my dad does until I finish Architecture school." Patrick appeared to mumble something under his breath.

"Sorry. I didn't catch what you said."

"I said when I eventually finish school, if I ever do."

Patrick appeared to relax a little, popping a fry into his mouth. "My parents own a small vineyard outside Half Moon Bay down the coast." he stated. "They wanted to open a city establishment to sell the wine, so Brodie's Bar was launched two years ago."

"So how did the bar get its name?" He had my attention now.

"Brodie is the family name. We're all Irish descendants." He looked over and smiled.

"I've had to put school on hold for the time being for Coco's sake. I need to spend every minute behind the bar at the moment."

"You're training to be an architect . . . and all the wine you sell is from your family's private label?" I gasped.

"Yep!" Patrick munched on his burger, wiping his lips with a napkin as he spoke.

"That's very impressive, Patrick."

"I'm earning my Sommelier certificate while working behind the bar, I guess I'll eventually get back to my Architectural Studies . . . one day." He turned and stared at me. "I'm a very busy guy, Willow."

Ouch! Touche.

I had him all wrong. *Never judge a book by its cover, Willow. You should know that by now.*

"How about I pour you a glass of the estate wine when we get back?"

I eased up. "I would love that! Thank you . . ."

Gosh, I had him all wrong.

"You ready to go?" he asked, putting his trash in the brown paper bag.

"Yes." I wiped my mouth one last time, throwing it in the bag. He took the bag from me, "Yes. Let's go."

Patrick reversed the Hilux and sped off to join the freeway into San Francisco. "We'll be at the Realty office in about ten minutes." He drew me a sideways look while swerving to avoid a car that was trying to overtake us on the inside lane.

"Realty office?"

"You know . . . to sign the papers."

"Oh . . . yes! Of course." I felt stupid but there were still some words in my American lexicon which were altogether unfamiliar to me.

"Back home we call it the Estate Agents." I clasped my hands on my lap and drew him a shrewd smile.

"Well you ain't *back home* now are you love?"

"No. I guess I'm not."

That's me put in my place.

I desperately wanted to ask him about his relationship with Carmen and wondered who Coco was.

Gosh, I had him all wrong.

The second part of the journey was a breeze as we drove past The Golden Gate Bridge with Marin County in the distance.

"Carmen lives over there." He indicated as we drove.

"Yes. I know."

I calculated that Marin County to Half Moon Bay was quite a distance. *Must be serious.* I thought.

Patrick pulled the Hilux up in front of a familiar looking street.

"Wait. I know this place. This is Lombard Street." I said. It was dark and the street was busy with traffic. Patrick smiled to himself as he parked up two doors away from Brodie's Bar.

"What?" he turned and stared at me. "I wanted to get to know you a little better. You seemed so uppity every time you came into the bar."

Uppity? Uppity? Who the hell is he calling uppity?

He took the keys out of his jacket pocket and opened up the door to a petite chic white boutique.

"The last tenant left last week." He declared as he stood in the centre of the shop.

"It's perfect!" I gasped.

"You like it? Good. You can have it at a 25% discount if you take the lease for six months."

I took the iPad out of my Kate Spade bag and began to photograph the interior just as Mrs. G. had instructed.

"There's enough room here for six work-stations." I counted the square footage with my feet, one foot in front of the other.

"Oh! And take a look at this!" Patrick walked towards the back of the shop and pulled back a curtained area to reveal a compact stainless steel galley kitchen, fitted with new appliances. He pointed at a sleek wine refrigerator, lined inside with a few leftover bottles of chilled chardonnay.

He leaned in closer. "The deal is that you must stock our private label wine and give it to your customers."

"I'm sure we can do that."

"And do you have a rat problem?" I chimed in.

"Clean as a whistle." He smiled.

"In that case, where do I sign?"

He looked at his watch. "We'll sign the lease back at Lancaster Realty. They look after all the family's real estate." He held the door open for me. "It's just around the corner from here, they'll be expecting us."

"But wait. They're open at this time of night? And what made you so sure I would sign?" I placed both hands on my hips and stared at him.

Patrick laughed to himself while shaking his head in disbelief.

"You don't have much time or many options--do you?" He stood in front of me, staring at me. "I called in a favour. Now let's get going."

"Um . . . no. I guess not." I sighed.

"And if all be told, it is pretty spot on for your needs, isn't it?" Patrick stared hard at me.

"OK. OK. No need to rub it in."

I began to feel on edge. "Right, let's go," I commanded, trying once again to gain the upper hand in the situation.

Patrick drew me one of his signature silent smiles, irritating me even more.

His smarmy tone was starting to annoy me once again.

Five minutes later we entered the entrance to Lancaster Realty. From the burnished metal placard on the front door, I read that the office was on the fifth floor of the old Victorian styled building.

"Do you want to walk or shall we take the elevator?" Patrick asked, looking me up and down as he spoke.

"I'm tired. Let's take the lift."

"You mean elevator." He smirked.

"No, I mean lift."

Patrick puffed his cheeks out in annoyance and pulled back the cast iron cage that enveloped the old-fashioned elevator.

"Your carriage awaits, madam."

I drew him a look as I entered. I wasn't fond of escalators or elevators and didn't have a head for heights. I pushed back against the side of the elevator and watched on as Patrick pulled the cage door shut. He looked over at me, indicating that I should press the button.

In silence, we rode up as the elevator creaked and rattled. I broke out in a cold sweat as I watched us climb higher and higher. I folded my arms and looked at my feet, trying to avoid the view that was visible from the wrought iron cage.

"God, I just want this to be over." I mumbled to myself as we climbed slowly towards the third floor. There was barely room for the two of us inside the capsule.

Patrick sighed. "Nearly there."

We passed up over the third floor on our way to the fourth when I heard a huge clunking sound.

"What the ?. . ."

The capsule came to a grinding halt as metal screeched on metal.

My stomach buckled. "No . . . "

"Calm down for Chrissakes . . ." Patrick reached over in front of me and pressed the fifth-floor button over and over . . . to no avail.

"What the fuck. We're stuck," he shouted.

"Talk about stating the obvious." I drew him a jaded look, indicating that I had reached that very conclusion long before he did.

Now it was his turn to lose as it as he pressed the alarm button over and over.

"How old is this thing?" He shouted.

I slid my back down the wall of the elevator and slumped onto the dusty floor. I no longer cared about the uniform I was wearing. It took another five or six minutes before Patrick joined me on the floor.

He folded his arms and looked over at me, staring intently. "Are you some kind of jinx? I mean do these kinds of things often happen to you."

"What kind of question is that to ask?" He had just succeeded in inflaming my temper even more. I scowled, daring him to respond.

Patrick realised he had overstepped the mark as he attempted to backtrack. "It's just that . . . well . . ."

"Well, what?" I said.

"Nothing like this has ever happened to me before." He stated, staring back at me.

I let out a snarly laugh and picked at an invisible speck on my tooth. "You haven't lived." I shook my head haughtily, folded my arms in defiance and stared straight ahead, willing for a hunky fireman to rescue me from this torture.

"Quite clearly, I have not." Patrick began to chuckle. "It's quite an adventure hanging out with you, Willow."

But my mind was elsewhere. Pressure was starting to build in my bladder and I needed to pee.

Patrick picked up on my silence.

"What's wrong with you."

As I sat on the floor, I crossed my legs. "Nothing." I attempted sweetness but it didn't work.

"There is something wrong," he stated, in that annoying way of his.

"No. There's not." I let out a small, worried sigh.

Patrick became silent, while I sweated.

I reckon five minutes passed before he spoke again.

"Do you want to play a game?" he asked, hopefully.

I sighed again. "No." Pressure was continuing to build below.

I crossed and re-crossed my legs, hoping in some way to maintain pressure down below, my discomfort growing by the second.

"How about I-Spy?" he asked.

"How about you shut up?" I responded. Patrick appeared wounded and I immediately regretted my obnoxious tone.

"Sorry."

Now's the time Willow. You've got to tell him before you pee your pants.

"Patrick."

"What?"

"I need to pee. Real bad."

He puffed out his cheeks once more and let out a huge sigh. "You're . . . You're killin' me Willow."

"That's not helpful Patrick. I need to pee." I brought my knees up carefully towards my chest as I made attempts to stand up, which was difficult seeing as I was exerting so much pressure down below. Patrick swooped down, put one arm under mine and pulled me up to full height. I smoothed my hair down, trying my best to maintain a small amount of composure. The sickly sensation of cold sweat ran down my spine.

"I don't have much time left, Patrick. We need to find a solution to this problem very quickly." I looked deep inside my bag for a receptacle of sorts that would be able to hold a quantity of liquid but couldn't find anything.

"I have just the thing." He stared blankly at me as he slurped the remainder of his huge coke through the straw. Once his cup was empty, he handed it to me.

"I'll eh . . . face the other way while you do . . . er."

I grabbed the cup from him, thanking him silently and waited while he turned his back.

Once the deed was done, I placed the almost full to the brim cup on the floor in the corner of the elevator.

"You can turn around now."

Patrick was grinning so hard, while my cheeks were aflame with embarrassment.

"I don't suppose you have a lid?"

***

The fire brigade turned up twenty-five minutes later and released us from our gilded birdcage. One of the firemen even offered to dispose of the offending cup for me but I told him I would get rid of it myself.

As I walked toward the Lancaster Realty office door, on the way back from the Ladies Powder Room, I wondered how I could ever face Patrick Brodie again.

Game face on Willow. Pretend like nothing happened.

I stared at the Broker, ignoring Patrick. "Now where do I sign."

***

Twenty minutes later, Patrick and I entered Brodie's Bar through the staff entrance. The hallway was crammed full of boxes of supplies and empty bottles piling up in a corner.

"'Scuse the mess." He rifled through a pile of papers that were piled high on his makeshift desk in the kitchen. I scanned the room, taking in the minute details of his working life.

"Could do with some organisation around here." I offered.

Patrick laughed. "It's a bit of a one-man show at the moment . . . staff turnover has been high." He grimaced. "Ah . . . found it." He pulled a maintenance checklist out from a messy bundle and offered it to me. "This tells you who the utility suppliers are and there's a list of

74

emergency contacts on there . . ." His eyes twinkled with mirth as he stared at me, "You know . . . in case you ever find yourself in a predicament again." His fingers brushed mine as he handed me the paperwork. I felt a small chill go up my spine. I grabbed the sheet of paper and turned my back on him, trying once again to keep my composure.

"Take a seat in the bar and I'll bring you a glass of our house special."

"Oh, OK." I smiled. I turned back towards the bar area and made myself at home in a corner booth. As I scanned the paperwork, I couldn't help but notice his easy way with his customers.

Dionne Warwick belted out the opening lines to "Do You Know The Way To San Jose?" over the bar's sound system.

Patrick brought over a large glass of the winery's special edition wine.

"Are you going to sit with me, while I look over the paperwork?" I looked up at him, hopefully.

He placed his hand, lightly, on my shoulder, and stared down at me. "Give me a moment, will you? There's a bit of a rush right now."

"No. I completely understand." I felt foolish. I took a sip of the delicious, chilled wine and exhaled loudly.

There was a flurry of activity at the entrance to the bar.

"Perfect timing. Here's Carmen." His face lit up. "I'll ask her to take over from me, while we look over the papers."

My heart sank at the mention of her name. I waved over as she took off her jacket and prepared to serve the customers.

I sipped a glass of wine and gently bit the tip of my pencil as I worked out new targets for the team. The new store was smaller and with a reduction in rent and not having to pay for the tab fees at Fred's, I worked out the overall costs would be reduced by 30% just by changing premises.

Mrs. G. will be over the moon. Not that she'll ever let me know.

Job well done. I gave myself an invisible congratulatory pat on the back as I watched Carmen and Patrick cozy up together. I realised that being on the road alone was full of adventure, excitement, and a certain kind of loneliness. I had no one to share my news with.

Ten minutes later. Patrick finally sat down opposite me. He took a sip from his glass of coke. He appeared harassed.

"Sorry I took so long. Couldn't get away. Carmen went to the mall with Coco . . . seems they got delayed on the way back."

"I see that. No worries, so business is good?"

Who the hell is Coco?

He stared at me, holding my gaze slightly longer than necessary. "It is now."

Fuck! My heart is racing. Keep your cool.

I smiled back at him. I could tell without looking that Carmen was looking over at us.

"Is everything to your liking?" he asked.

"What do you mean?" I shifted awkwardly on the banquette, not quite sure where to look.

"The paperwork!" he laughed.

"Oh that . . . yeah. Everything is fine. Perfectly fine." I scratched the top of my head, making a vain attempt to remain unflustered.

He leaned over to shake my hand. His grip was tight and steady. His hand was hot.

"Welcome aboard."

"Thank you," I beamed. We locked eyes.

Carmen interrupted. I didn't realise she was with us. She stood behind Patrick, placing her arms around his neck.

"Hi Willow." She beamed.

The moment was gone.

"Hi Carmen."

I stood up and gathered my things.

"Bye Carmen." I smiled as I walked away. "I'll see you at half-past nine tomorrow." But Carmen didn't hear me--she was busy whispering something to Patrick. Patrick stood up and rushed off towards the bar.

"Be back in a minute." He called.

But I was already making my way towards the door.

For a fleeting second or two, I imagined Carmen walking down the rose-lined aisle at the homestead winery in Half Moon Bay, the Californian sun hitting off her high, bronzed cheekbones as she kissed Patrick.

Get a grip, Willow!

Back in my hotel room, my phone pinged.

It was Mrs. G. She had made arrangements for the boutique décor to be removed from the first boutique to the second. And that I needed to be in attendance all day tomorrow to oversee the layout and interior design.

I looked around at the cold, empty hotel room and sensed my mood spiral downwards. I felt tired and stressed and faintly disappointed.

Where's Jackson when you need him?

The phone pinged again. I sighed. *What is it this time?*

> "WHY DID YOU RUSH OFF WITHOUT SAYING GOODBYE?

I texted back:

> WHO IS THIS?
>
> PAT!
>
> HOW DID YOU GET MY NUMBER?
>
> IT WAS ON THE LEASE!

I threw myself down on top of the bed and hugged the pillow to my face. I liked him. I had to admit it to myself. But I knew I could never be that girl. The type of girl who steals another woman's man.

A mild flirtation is what this is. That's all. I'll be flying back to New York next week and I won't give Patrick Brodie a second thought.

Thoughts flitted in and out of my mind at break-neck speed.

You're a career woman now Willow. You don't need another man messing up your life. Mrs. G. is depending on you to make a success of the stores. He lives in San

Francisco. You're an international jet setter. AND HE'S WITH CARMEN!

I didn't respond.

CHAPTER SEVEN

Crossed Wires & Cabernet

The next few days passed in a blur as I stood in attendance at the new store, overseeing the carpentry work and making design decisions with the interior decorator. I did my best to keep the carpenters sweet by going on coffee errands. Keeping them fuelled up on caffeine was my main objective, while I sought to keep the hot but annoying barman out of my thoughts.

On one coffee run, I stood in line inside a quaint roast house, waiting patiently on my order, when outside a familiar-looking figure caught my attention.

Is that him?

I squinted through the glass at the man standing on the sidewalk, holding a little girl's hand.

It can't be. It does look like him though . . .

They were dressed in warm clothing while the little girl wore a backpack over her school blazer.

My eyes did a double-take as I scanned over our previous conversations. I recalled he had mentioned someone called Coco.

Is that Coco? Is that her?

"Ma'am, your order for Plane Jane's is ready."

I turned to face the assistant. "Thanks!" but by the time I had grabbed the coffee holder and splashed some of the cups' contents over my hand and exited the roast house, the man and the little girl were gone. I stood on the sidewalk and scanned the street but there was no sign of them.

"I'm a very busy man, Willow." He had said. I turned and walked back towards the store, deep in thought, mulling his words over and over.

Is my sullen bartender a strung-out daddy? And if so, who's the mother?

Back at the store, I slunk into the kitchen and sat down on one of the chairs nestled under the table. I couldn't get to Google quick enough to do a search on Patrick Brodie, but as hard as I searched nothing came up. Google was only giving me the information I already knew.

Who is this bloody man of mystery?

I caught myself thinking of him again and quickly brought myself back to the here and now. *Carmen knows everything.*

I took another gulp of the coffee.

But if I ask her it will be too obvious and then it'll spoil our work relationship.

I snapped myself out of my mental chaos and brought myself back to the here and now. I checked the time and made some quick calculations. There were only two and a half days left till we re-launched and the relentless onslaught of orders from Mrs. G. continued to pour fast.

I did a double-take on her last message.

"Fresh eucalyptus branches displayed in empty milk bottles in the customer bathroom, darling! And a diffuser filled with sage and geranium essential oils to ward off any lingering evil spirits."

I stood up and placed the cup in the trash, shaking my head in disgust.

Woman has clearly lost the plot now.

I made my way out towards the local farmer's market to search for old-fashioned milk bottles and out-of-season eucalyptus branches.

***

The 'second' launch of the San Francisco Plane Jane Beauty boutique went without a hitch.

When I arrived at the premises, Carmen was already present and had arranged for everyone to be in attendance. Josefina was applying more lipstick to Jesse and Finn was talking to a customer on the store phone. I recognised there and then that I had chosen well, Carmen was an awesome store manager, and I was more than happy to leave her in charge of the pop-up.

As expected, the press didn't turn up. They already had their big scoop on us and had refused to come back for a second review. *I mean who could blame them really?* I estimated that only half of the original lineup of clients made it to the store that morning, but we had invited enough people inside the tiny boutique to make it look busy. I took photos on the iPad and emailed them to Mrs. G. so that she could post on the Plane Jane Beauty social media channels. It was apparent that word was getting out. San Francisco had a new beauty parlour in town making us interesting enough to be visited by some of the city's leading lifestyle influencers.

Finn tapped me on the shoulder.

"This message just came in from George in New York." He indicated for me to look at his phone.

Jasmine Buckley. Instagram following 55k. Beauty Blogger arriving sometime in the next hour. Might be undercover or she might make herself known. This is what she looks like. Be on the lookout. Treat her like royalty.

Yours Truly

George

Sparkle PR Productions

New York, New York

"Aww, this is all we need." I said, staring at Finn.

"I did a search on her." His eyes glinted with mirth.

"You're a rock star, Finn. She's all yours."

"Thank you," he said.

I could tell he was up for the challenge.

Whatever Jasmine Buckley wants, she can have.

It wasn't too long before Finn got his opportunity to take care of the blogger. He recognised her as soon as she stepped in the store. She wore a huge sun hat and a 1950s style blue and white polka dot dress combined with gigantic pearls and red shiny shoes. On her arm, she carried a beige Burberry raincoat and a statement umbrella, the kind that Mary Poppins would have carried. Undercover or not undercover, she stood out a mile.

"Oh my gosh," she said as she entered the store. Finn greeted with her a glass of fizz.

"Welcome aboard the Plane Jane Beauty Flight." He indicated for her to take a seat at the check-in desk while he took her details. I looked on as he navigated his way through the procedure, handing her a boarding card for her appointment.

"You'll be seated in seat 2a and I will be performing your makeover."

Jasmine was clearly excited that Finn would be doing her makeup. I waited till she was seated and comfortable before going over to check in on her.

"Hi Miss Buckley. I'm the COO of Plane Jane Beauty. We're all delighted you are here today."

Jasmine batted her huge eyelashes as she looked up at me.

"My pleasure. I heard so much about you guys I just had to come in and see for myself what all the fuss is about."

"Fabulous. Well, I'll leave you in the capable hands of Finn. If you need anything at all just let me know." I gushed, layering on the customer service.

When her appointment was over, and she was fully made up, it was time to take some photos with the beauty blogger. Carmen called through to Brodie's to ask Patrick to come into the store and take a group photo of us all. I watched as Jasmine threw her arms around him, almost knocking him off his feet.

"Whoa! Steady, lady!" He threw me a sideways look and shook his head. I laughed a little as Jasmine kissed him on either cheek.

"Paddy! I missed you babes!"

Patrick appeared to blush slightly as Jasmine showered him with affection.

"OK! OK! Calm down."

I guessed being a local bartender had its benefits. I decided to take charge of the situation.

"Jasmine! Stand over here between Carmen and I, will you?"

Patrick nodded a silent 'thank you' as I directed her over towards me. We all stood in line with Jasmine taking centre stage, posing in a way that showed she was accomplished at having her photograph taken. The rest of us were lined up in our Plane Jane Beauty uniforms.

I prayed that everything had gone to plan and that she got the photos she needed for her blog. Carmen gave her the biggest gift bag we could find and crammed it to overflowing with items from the beauty brand collection. After she had left in a flurry of hype and activity, I went over to thank Patrick.

"I owe you one."

"You certainly do," he gasped, eyes twinkling at me.

He looked up at me with a dazed look on his face.

"Swing by the bar tonight at closing time and you can buy me a drink."

"Closing time! That's way too late for me. I'll be sound asleep by then." I said.

Patrick looked disappointed. He slung his hands into his jean pockets and turned to leave.

"Right. I better get back to the bar."

He seemed annoyed that I didn't take him up on his offer but my attention was required elsewhere.

Finn tapped me on the shoulder, "I guess I'm really going to enjoy working here." He said, staring up at me like the cat that had just gotten the cream.

"What's the matter? What's happened?"

"Jasmine just sent me a text asking me to help her out at a fashion show in LA next week! Is that OK with you? It's not a conflict of interest, is it?" He asked, a concerned look on his face, that he might miss his big moment.

"Not if you're going along to represent our brand." I said, my business brain was working overtime. "Make that part of the agreement and I'll give you time to go down there."

He leaned in and hugged me. "Thanks, Willow." I could tell he was brimming with excitement at the prospect.

Later that afternoon, after I had gone over store targets and carried out a cleanliness check on the premises, I sat in the back room with Carmen.

"OK. We need to check we have enough supplies in stock."

I scanned the store cupboard shelves making quick calculations in my head.

"We appear to have enough of the brand supplies. I want you to serve champagne to our customers every weekend." I stepped back into the kitchen and checked the wine refrigerator." We only had a few bottles of fizz left.

"I'm just going to pop next door and order a few more bottles from Brodie's."

I checked my reflection in the mirror. My stomach was full of nervous anticipation as I stepped out of the beauty parlour. I strode towards the bar and peered inside. It was empty. I observed Patrick reading a newspaper. The customary black and white gingham tea towel he usually wore was still over one shoulder. I noticed he glanced up at me as I entered. He drew me a weird kind of look then walked away.

Cheeky git! Just because I didn't accept his offer of a drink . . . now he's ignoring me?

I waited. And waited.

"Yoo hoo! Is anyone there?" I called through to the back room. "I'm waiting." I tapped the company credit card on top of the bar, indicating my impatience.

Patrick made an appearance.

"What do you want?" he stared at me. I couldn't quite analyse the expression on his face, but I guess he was a little mad.

"I need a small order of champagne, please." My tone of voice equalled his.

He took out his notebook and grabbed the Biro which appeared to be always stuck behind his right ear.

"How many?" he sighed.

"I think six should do it for now. Six bottles of the signature label please." I handed over the credit card as he tallied up the sale. His expression was devoid of any emotion. I stared back in equal measure, refusing to be intimidated by his coldness.

He handed back the credit card.

"Thank you very much."

"I'll bring the bottles through when I get a break." He went back to reading his newspaper.

I felt stupid and self-conscious. "Oh. I see. Thank you." I looked around the empty bar then I turned and walked towards the doorway wishing with every ounce of me that I had texted the order instead.

"I get the impression you're annoyed with me?" the words blurted out of my mouth before I could stop them.

"Annoyed? No." He stared straight at me, holding my gaze. "Confused? Yes." He shook his head as he rubbed away an invisible mark on the bar. "I thought we were getting on well?"

I shifted my weight from foot to foot, I frowned as I stared back at him. "It's you who's being weird, not me." I replied.

"How come?" he placed both hands on his hips as he stared back. He really did look confused.

"It's just that . . . I'm just so *not* in the mood to be going for a drink with a guy who already has a girlfriend." I stated, then turned to leave. "It's just not my style."

Patrick closed his newspaper, "Wait! Hold on. What do you mean?

Girlfriend?"

I stopped in my tracks then turned to face him. Now it was my turn to shake my head. "Oh don't give me that, Patrick. You know fine well I'm talking about Carmen."

"Carmen?" he scratched his head, as a huge smile spread across his face. "You think Carmen and I are going out?" He slung his hands deep down into his pockets and looked around the room, before staring at me. "You crack me up, lady," he said, laughing.

Now it was my turn to feel unsure of myself.

"Carmen Monaco is my baby cousin." He stated. "Occasionally, she helps out in the bar." He took out his phone and showed me the screen. It was an image of him and Carmen and other family members at the launch of Brodie's Winery two years ago.

Bloody hell, Willow. You got this so wrong.

I stared at him, then at the phone screen again then back at him.

"Oops!"

"So that's why you didn't respond." His sentence was a cross between a statement and a question.

I said nothing.

Just then the little black Papillon came bounding out from behind the bar and rushed first towards Patrick then towards me.

I bent down to stroke her. "Thanks Lola," I said, under my breath, grateful that the dog had caused a distraction and a break in the tension.

Eventually Patrick smiled at me. "I think she likes you."

I smiled back at Patrick, relieved and happy that we had cleared up the Carmen misunderstanding, but I felt unsure on how to proceed.

"I think she has very good taste," I replied.

That's it, Willow. Get your sass back.

Patrick took a step towards me. "So Lola and I are going for a walk at lunchtime--would you care to join us?"

I checked my watch. "I think that could be arranged."

Back in the store, I made straight for the kitchen and caught Carmen just as she was finishing her tea-break.

"Why didn't you tell me?"

"Tell you what?" Carmen asked.

"Tell me that Patrick is your cousin!"

"Why would I tell you that?" Carmen stared at me for a second or two. "Oh! I see." She smiled.

"You like him!" She began to giggle.

I held my finger up at my mouth to shush her.

"Don't worry. Everyone already guessed that you liked him. I mean, he can't stay away from you."

"What do you mean?"

"Well . . . haven't you noticed he comes into the beauty parlour every opportunity he gets?" she asked.

"No. I hadn't noticed that."

We locked eyes and began to laugh.

"OK. Now I get it." I relented, my mind flicking over all the times that Patrick had come into the pop-up store.

"So? Are you going to go out with him. Please say yes and put us all out of our misery."

"We're going for a walk with the dog at lunchtime," I replied haughtily, smiling at Carmen as I spoke.

"Thank God for that!" she declared. "He's been driving me bonkers, asking me questions about you. Oh, and by the way, you saw him outside the coffee store the other morning?"

"Yes?"

"That was a set up." She laughed. "I told him you would be popping out for coffee before coming into work."

I slapped her playfully on the arm. "Carmen!"

"Just want my big cousin to be happy, that's all!" she stated, as she walked away. "I couldn't think of anyone nicer for him to go out with."

"Thanks. That means a lot."

Carmen looked at her watch. "You've got half an hour . . . do you want me to touch up your makeup . . . you're looking a little flustered. Here take a seat. Let me work my magic."

***

I strode up to the entrance to Brodie's Bar where Patrick stood waiting for me. He held Lola on a short leash but, even still, she attempted to jump up on my flight attendant's uniform the second she realized who I was.

"Sorry about that." Patrick pulled her back as I neared him.

"It's OK." I smiled, unsure of how to proceed.

I mean, is this even a date or are we just going for a walk?

I guessed that Patrick sensed my nerves as he held out a hand to me. "May I?" He had changed out of his earlier outfit and had made an attempt with his hair. The sun shone off his gold aviators as I offered my hand. I was glad that he was taking control of the situation, leaving me in no doubt that we were on a 'date.'

He squeezed my hand in his as we walked along the sidewalk. It was a comforting squeeze.

"You look very smart," he said.

"I didn't have any option but to wear this. All my outfits are in the hotel." I felt slightly stupid walking down the street, suited and booted in my aviation gear. Lola had positioned herself squarely between us as we walked. We must have made quite the spectacle walking down the street as others looked on. But I didn't care.

"We can just go along here to the park." Patrick indicated as we passed the same coffee shop we had bumped into each other earlier in the week. I pulled on his hand.

"Hold on a minute. Do you want a latte to take to the park?" I chirped. "I know how you like your coffee." I knew I was being cheeky but carried on. "Carmen told me you had set up the whole 'bumping into me at the coffee shop' thing the other day." I laughed. Patrick looked like he was blushing.

"She did, did she? Wait till I see her."

"It's OK. I'm very flattered." I grinned. I recalled the number of times I had 'bumped' into Patrick Brodie in the last week and there had been 5 occasions.

Had they all been engineered?

"Hold the leash, will you?" Patrick entered the small café and ordered two coffees. He also ordered two glazed donuts. Then we set off for the park.

We walked into Fay Park. "Do you mind if we sit here?" I asked. "These shoes are killing me."

"Sure thing. Take a seat." He extended his arm indicating for me to sit down, then he snuggled up close to me, handing me the coffee and the donut. I noticed he placed one arm along the back of the bench. I set my bag down on the gravel and pulled out my pair of Repetto ballet pumps. I sensed Patrick stare at me as I changed out the shoes.

"That's better." I said, smiling.

"Do you always do that?" he asked.

"What?"

"Carry a spare pair of shoes with you everywhere you go?"

"Mostly . . . yes!" I rubbed the heel of my right foot.

"You women are crazy! You would never catch a guy doing that sort of thing," he said.

"Well, you guys don't normally walk around in three-inch heels, do you?" I said.

"You never know . . . I might have a thing." His mouth creased into a smile and I smiled back. I was warming to *this* Patrick. He was easy on the eye and comfortable to be around. I felt at ease with him. Like I could laugh and joke and jest with him and nothing would become an issue.

Reign it in Willow. You're falling too fast . . . as per bloody usual.

I smiled inwards while my stomach rolled with nerves. Only this time it was a good feeling.

He turned and looked at me. "So. Willow. Finally, I have you all to myself." He stared at me for a moment before erupting into a huge smile, "barring our little elevator situation of course!"

"Let's not talk about that." I couldn't think of anything else to say. I felt as awkward as hell, my nerves were thrust into top gear. He pressed his knees against mine as we sat on the park bench, both of us staring at Lola.

"Have you lost your tongue?" I asked, giggling.

Is Patrick Brodie losing his cool? I wondered.

He looked up at the sky. "I can see it now . . . a reporter asking, "well Patrick Brodie . . . how did you meet Willow Campbell?"

"Well, there was a situation with a stuck elevator and an empty cup of coke." He looked upwards and chuckled to himself as if he was reading some kind of huge newspaper in the sky.

He turned to look at me, shaking his head. "I just can't believe you said 'yes' to me. I'm still getting over the shock."

"Oh! Away with you!" I blushed, feeling like I was back in high school, being asked out by a boy. He held my hand and stared at me.

"Will you come out with me tonight? After work? I'd like to take you for a drink . . . somewhere away from the bar." His green eyes glinted.

"Yes. I would like that." Perhaps my response shot from my mouth faster than I would have liked, but part of me didn't care. I liked Patrick Brodie and he had just told me that he liked me . . . a lot.

He stood up and held out his hand to pull me up from the park bench. "Come over here," he said, "I want to show you the sundial."

I walked over with him and stood opposite the dial. He read the inscription aloud, "grow old with me, the best is yet to be." The hairs on my arms bristled as I observed him stare at the inscription.

"This place is so charming." I felt as awkward as hell, trying to change the subject. "Can you imagine growing old with anyone, being with the same person your whole life? Like never wanting to be with anyone else?" Patrick stared at the sundial as he rubbed his chin, deep in thought. I regretted asking the question.

He turned and stared at me. "I did once."

I noticed Patrick's mood appeared to change slightly.

"It's a miracle anyone stays together these days!" He turned to look at me. "Sorry. That wasn't a jab at you and that Rick guy."

I felt kind of foolish, like I had to explain myself. "That was my fault." I stated. "You know that song? *Only fools rush in'* by the Mamas and Papas? Well . . . that fool was me."

Patrick took my hand as we walked. "Don't be so self-deprecating. We've all done stupid things, Willow. No-one's perfect."

"What about you? Have you ever rushed into a relationship?" I asked, finally glad to have the opportunity to get the focus off myself.

"Nowadays, I'm more of the slow, cautious type, I guess." He pulled Lola away from another approaching dog. "It can take me a while to warm up to people. I like to analyse from behind the bar."

"Yeah. I noticed that."

"You did?" He looked surprised.

"So, we're like yin and yang," I laughed. "I'm trying to learn to be more like you."

This stopped him in his tracks. "No. Please don't do that! Stay the way you are. I like you . . . just the way you are." His eyes lingered on mine a moment longer than necessary. I felt like I could see through to his soul.

"You do?" I felt slightly shocked yet elated.

"Don't you change for anyone. That's an order!"

I mulled over what he said, smiling to myself as we walked on in silence.

I like this Patrick Brodie.

Patrick broke the silence. "I come here most days, with Lola. It's so peaceful. A nice break from all the hustle and bustle."

"The landscaping is gorgeous. So pretty." We locked eyes again. Patrick stepped in closer and held me lightly around the waist.

"May I?" said Patrick.

I nodded and giggled. No man had ever asked my permission to kiss me. This was a first for me.

He lowered his head and kissed me in front of the sundial. It was a serene kiss. Gentle and tender. I felt slightly embarrassed to be kissing him in broad daylight in the middle of the park, but eventually I got over myself as his lips enveloped mine. Seconds later, he pulled away from me and smiled.

"We best get back to work then." He stated as he called Lola over.

Lola took up her stance in the space between us.

"I think she likes you . . . a lot," said Patrick.

Our short date had been perfect. I held back slightly to change back into my heels as Patrick walked on ahead, calling Lola to him. When I eventually caught up with them, which was difficult in my heeled shoes, he held both my hands and pulled me towards him.

"What are you doing?" I giggled nervously.

I thought he was going to kiss me again! Right there in the middle of the street in broad daylight.

"Just clench your teeth together a minute," he said.

"Why?"

He pulled the sleeve of his sweater over his finger then raised his hand to my face.

"Now smile," he ordered.

What the? . . . What is he up to? . . .

He traced the top of his finger over my top row of teeth.

"That's it. All gone now. You had speckles. Red lipstick."

But then he stepped closer and pulled me in tight towards him. He planted his pillowy lips on mine, taking me by surprise as he kissed me in the middle of the street. When I eventually pulled away, I noticed that Lola had sat herself down on top of his shoes, claiming her territory.

He flicked his hand out then pulled the leash tight as we set off down the street towards Brodie's and the beauty parlour.

Patrick Brodie had gotten his confidence back as he waved, "I'll see you at 11:00 pm at the bar."

What are you getting yourself into now, girl?

I turned to step back into the beauty parlour just as my phone sprung to life. It was Mrs. G.

"I've changed my mind. I think we ought to have white tulips." She texted.

I didn't care. She could have tulips from every bloody colour in the rainbow.

"White tulips it is, Mrs. Gerson." I replied.

New York was closing business for the day and there were 21 separate text messages making up one giant to-do list for me. As I scanned and read her instructions, I wondered if I would ever get away to meet Patrick for that drink.

"What's up?" Carmen asked. "Didn't it go well?" she looked concerned as she spoke.

But I was distracted by one message in particular. "What?" I glanced briefly at Carmen.

"Your date with Pat!"

"Oh . . . um, yeah! Can you hold court for twenty minutes? I've got to go back out. Gigi needs me to find her tulips in the colour of Ghirardelli Chocolate . . ." I headed out.

Carmen looked perplexed as I shot back out the door, up the street towards Brodies.

I walked in and called out, "Patrick, are you there?"

"So keen to see me so soon . . . I like your style Willow Campbell."
Patrick walked towards me. His hands slung low in his pockets and customary tea towel over one shoulder.

I showed Pat the message on my phone screen. I watched his expression change to one of disappointment as he looked at me then back at the screen.

"I guess tonight's date is cancelled then?"

I nodded my head. "Looks like it."

He stretched his hand out over the bar and touched my hand. "When will you be back."

"I . . . er . . . I don't know."

Patrick sighed. "That sucks." He threw the tea towel over his shoulder. "Go and do what you need to do. Your job is important."

"I don't believe this." I searched his eyes with mine, silently communicating my disappointment. "She's bringing the launch of the London store forward . . . and I've hardly had time here to get things up and running."

I threw my hands up in the air in frustration as Patrick continued to serve his customer. "She changes her mind every five minutes . . . I can't keep up with her requests. I mean one minute she wants orange flowers then she wants white! My head's going around in circles with her demands . . . and to top it all she wants chocolate-coloured tulips . . . I mean, what the hell?"

He shook his head, placing an arm around my shoulder. "The lady's got a business to run. I suppose you've got to do what she asks you to do." He stretched his hand out over the bar top and placed it on top of mine. He rubbed the top of my knuckles with his thumb as he stared at me. "We can make an arrangement to meet up in New York or something." He looked hopeful as he attempted to cheer me up. That suggestion raised my spirits for all of a few seconds.

"I was really starting to enjoy my time here . . . with you." I gave

Patrick a weak smile. I had to let him know how I felt.

"When do you leave?" he asked.

I checked my watch. "Making time for traffic . . . I guess I'll need to go back to my hotel, pack then leave here at 5:00 pm."

Patrick's face fell. "Oh well. So this *really* is goodbye." He grabbed my hand, placed it in his and bowed his head. "This has to be the shortest romance on record." He laughed a little, masking his own disappointment.

"Can I have a hug before you leave?" He pulled me towards him. I guessed the customers in the bar were looking over. He clutched on to me and held me tight, as Barbara Streisand sang the opening lines to *'Woman in Love.'*

"Can I see you again?"

The music, the lyrics, the atmosphere . . .

It felt like the beginning of something new and exciting. I didn't want to let him go.

I kissed him. "You have my number." I replied, then I pulled away and left Brodie's Bar for the final time.

On the way back to my hotel, I frantically texted George.

Have you heard the news?

I have to leave for New York tonight.

George replied in an instant.

I guess you're disappointed at having to leave San Francisco so soon?

We're all feeling the pressure, Wills. Did you enjoy your trip?

I responded.

Yes. The people are so nice!

George texted back.

Anyone special?!!

I paused a moment. I had never met George, but he seemed so kind and lovely.

Yes! Only been on one date.

George responded.

Good for you dear. Everyone needs a little happiness in their lives.

***

An hour later, I returned to the Beauty Parlour and set my belongings down in the designated baggage area. I was exhausted from all the toing and froing. I had a broken nail and my hair was unkempt.

"Look after Jesse for me, will you?" I asked, hair falling into my face as I scanned the boutique looking for products that were out of place.

Carmen nodded her head.

"But you're leaving so soon?"

"Yes. My boss has summoned me back to New York. Urgent business." I drew Carmen a sideways look, insinuating my displeasure at having to leave so abruptly.

"Does Jesse have anywhere to stay yet?" Carmen asked, clutching her coffee cup.

"No. She will need a few more nights in the hotel, then we will have to move her out. Between you and me, I've already tried to conceal the hotel bill from my boss-she won't be happy when she finds out about this." I grimaced, visualizing Mrs. G's reaction.

"Don't worry." Carmen placed her manicured hand on top of mine. "I have a close friend who rents a room out in her house. I'll figure something out." Carmen took out her phone and texted her friend.

"Thanks, Carmen. Much appreciated." Relieved, I picked up the iPad. "Let's go onto the shop floor and do a quick last-minute check."

***

I walked over to the cash register and ran some totals on the till all the while trying to get that last vision of Patrick out of my mind.

Takings are good. Mrs. G. will be pleased.

All in all, our second opening had been a great success on paper, and I could sense my team's confidence grow as a result.

So why do I feel like this inside?

I called the crew over to the curtained-off area and poured them each a glass of Brodie's fizz.

"To Plane Jane Beauty!" I raised my glass to clink it against the others. "So wonderful to meet you all." I forced out a smile. "I'm happy to say that we've smashed our targets for the day.

We're almost $2000 ahead with still four selling hours to go!"

The team hollered and hugged each other.

"I got each of you a Plane Jane Beauty gift card, so I want you to choose $75 worth of products to add to your personal kits." I handed the small white cards to each staff member.

"Carmen, make sure everyone gets something they can wear. Something that matches the uniform," I said and lifted up one of the brand's red lipsticks. "The Mile High Club goes great with the uniform."

"Now . . . I'm not sure when I'll be back," I said, smiling sadly, "as I have to launch the New York and London stores--" A few of the girls gasped.

I saw Jesse shift her body uncomfortably.

"Jesse, I'll try to fly you over to the New York store for training." I checked the time.

"Whoops! Time for me to go." I gestured as I gathered my belongings and made my way towards the door. "Now you know you can contact me by email," I called out, opening the door, "I might take a little time to respond to you, depending on time zones, but if the question is super urgent, Carmen is your first point of contact."

Carmen rushed towards the door to help me with my bags.

"Thanks," I said. "A taxi should be waiting for me."

"Oh, never mind the taxi." Carmen drew me a cheeky look. "Pat asked me to call him and let him know when you were ready to leave," Carmen said, as she pressed his number on her phone." She looked up at me as she spoke. "Pat! She's ready!" Carmen yelled into the receiver.

"It's really OK. I can get a taxi." I whispered as I struggled with my bags.

"Patrick Brodie is a very busy man. He told me so." Carmen waved her hand in the air. I wanted to make it a clean getaway, but she was having none of it.

I blushed as Patrick waited outside in the shiny red Hilux. He got out of the car, walked around and opened the passenger door for me. This was not how I envisioned leaving San Francisco.

"Your carriage awaits, ma'am."

Once seated in the Hilux, I called out to the team members standing in the doorway, "Goodbye!"

Alone inside the vehicle, I pressed on. "You really didn't need to do this. I was fine with getting a taxi."

His green eyes met mine. "What? And miss out on another opportunity to be with you? No chance, lady!"

I laughed as he gripped my hand in his, while putting the Hilux into reverse.

The journey to San Francisco International Airport took twenty minutes, but sitting side by side, mostly in heavily underpinned silence with only Dionne Warwick singing, "With a dream in your heart, you're never alone . . . ' I prayed we would hit every red light en route to the airport.

He remembered I liked Dionne Warwick.

I smiled to myself while staring straight ahead. Conversation seemed pointless as little sparks of electricity pirouetted around and under us as we sat in our seats.

Pull yourself together, Willow. You've only been on one mini-date. Quit behaving like a love struck schoolgirl. Didn't you learn anything from the Rick fiasco? You're a serious businesswoman now, so start acting like it!

As Patrick pulled up into a drop-off area, he finally spoke.

"When will you be back in town?"

"I have no idea." It was the truth.

Patrick turned his body towards me, speaking softly, "I'm flying to New York in a few weeks' time--it's a wine thing."

I unclipped the seat belt and made my way out of the wagon. I walked around to the driver's side and looked up at Patrick. "Perhaps I can take you out for that beer?" He looked hopeful as he stared at me.

"I think I'd like that." I blurted before my inner Editor had a chance to speak. "Although I don't drink beer . . . only wine."

"Well then," He gave me a crooked smile and a salute. "I'll bring you some of the own label red from the winery." He looked over my shoulder. "It looks very busy in there . . . just wish we had more time to get to know each other."

I nodded my head in agreement a little too vigorously.

"Yes . . . me too, Patrick."

"Look. For God's sakes just call me Pat, will ya?"

"No. I prefer to give people their full names." I stated.

Patrick laughed at me. "You're funny Willow." He reached his arm out the window and tapped my shoulder. "So old-fashioned . . . but I like it." He winked.

That annoyed me. "No. I'm not." My voice sounded so full of indignation. He climbed out of the Hilux, fetched my belongings from the back of the wagon then stood in front of me.

"Yes. You are." He bowed his head and kissed me on the lips. It was a long, lingering meaningful kiss. One that left me feeling slightly breathless as he pulled away.

"Safe flight."

He saluted then got back in the Hilux and revved up the engine. I held my green Kate Spade bag in front of me as I watched him drive off.

"Goodbye, Patrick Brodie." I whispered.

I turned and walked towards the check-in area, meandering through couples and families greeting each other. A gamut of emotions railroaded their way through my mind as I thought of Patrick.

Would he really fly in and meet me in New York or was it all just a mild flirtation? Only time will tell.

I checked in for the flight and navigated my way across the concourse, looking at design magazines in the local airport shops. It was a five-hour flight to New York and my stomach was rumbling. Passing by an artisan Bagel store, I popped in and took a pew at the patio area. I ordered a lox bagel, a latte and perused my magazine. Boarding would start any minute now. My thoughts were racing as my mind flitted over past events in San Francisco. On the surface, the trip had been a huge success. It had been everything I could ever have imagined from a business perspective: a fantastic team to work with, great sales figures, a stunning location in the centre of a hip, happening city but underneath all of this glam and fabulosity, I couldn't help but feel kind of hollow inside.

What's keeping me from feeling so happy?

I cupped my chin as I circled the spoon in my cup of frothy latte as I observed friends and lovers say their goodbyes. I smiled as I watched little children run to be re-united with an absent parent.

Success truly was a difficult beast to define.

"Is this seat taken?"

The familiarity of the voice got my attention. I looked up. Patrick Brodie was staring back at me.

"Oh! You came back!" I blurted. "Did you forget something?" My voice sounded harsh as I placed the coffee cup on the table, hoping he wouldn't see my hand tremble.

"I . . . er . . . brought you these." He handed me a tiny bunch of miniature chocolate-coloured tulips. His face fell as I started laughing. "It was all they had in stock at this time of day . . . in fact, I think these were headed for the trash."

"I guess I own you an apology."

I folded my arms across my body and stared over his shoulder.

"For what?" I asked.

"For calling you old-fashioned."

Patrick began to laugh.

"What's so funny?"

He sat down opposite me.

"You crack me up Willow--I've never met anyone quite like you before."

I didn't know exactly how to take that but I listened to his words.

Patrick's expression turned serious. "Look. I'm not going to waste any more time . . . The fact is I like you. I really like you. I liked you the first moment you walked into my bar.

His honesty took me off-guard.

"I know you have to fly to New York tonight." He put his hand over his mouth then paused, "But I wondered if you might consider staying in San Francisco for one more day?"

I was shocked by his directness. I sat in silence as he stared at me, awaiting my response.

"I don't know what to say . . . You've really taken me by surprise, Patrick . . . um I mean Pat."

"Well, that's a step forward--you calling me Pat." He smiled, relaxing a little. That was then I realized how difficult all this must be for him.

I fumbled with my plate, as I took in what he had just asked me to do. I was shocked and unnerved and taken completely off-guard, but if I was really honest with myself, I was also flattered.

"Can I--" I swallowed, "can I have a moment to think about this?" I asked, staring over at him.

Patrick looked at me, "Of course you can--I'll wait over there." He pointed to the huge flight departure board. He pushed back his chair and stood up to full height.

Once he was gone, I let out a huge sigh.

"Jesus, Mary and Joseph!" I mumbled to myself in my very bad Irish accent that appeared automatically as soon as I uttered those words. My heart raced and the palms of my hands sweated as I mulled over his suggestion.

Where's Jackson when I need him? Where's my yellow book?

I didn't have any props with me. All I had was my gut sensation. I stared over at the departure board at the sweetest man I had laid eyes on. I observed him from a distance as he paced up and down amidst the throng of passengers milling in front of the board.

My mind flitted over all of our brief interactions. Meeting him for the first time in the bar, thinking that he and Carmen were 'an item', that fateful trip to the Realty office. I shuddered at the memory of that. The walk in the park with him and his beautiful Lola . . . the burger in the parking lot.

George! Text George!

I pulled out my phone and composed a message to George:

George! Quick question: The lovely man I was telling you about has just asked me to stay one more day in San Francisco. What should I do?

I pressed send then clasped my hands together and said a silent prayer. George was always prompt with his replies. I watched on as Patrick paced up and down, then bristled with anxiety as I heard the final boarding call for my departing flight on the airport tannoy. I had to make a decision . . . now.

My phone pinged. I let out a sigh of relief. It was George. He had responded.

Wills. Fortune favours the bold. If you want to stay one more day, I will cover for you.

I let out a gasp. I couldn't believe I was going to do this.

I responded to the text.

I owe you one. Thank you!

"This is a final call for all passengers on the JetBlue 616 flight to New York JFK. Please go to Gate B6 where your flight is waiting to depart."

I pushed back my chair and walked determinedly in the direction of

Patrick. Thoughts did battle in my mind. *Can I trust my gut when I was so wrong before? I married Rick after a six-week romance, how stupid can you be?*

I recalled a quote from my yellow book as I glanced over at Pat, "If it's both terrifying and amazing, pursue it."

Slowly, I walked towards him. He didn't notice me amidst the crowd. I tugged on his arm.

"Twenty-four hours you said?"

"Uh-huh." Patrick smiled back, his eyes darting across my face, scanning my expression for clues, a lock of dirt blonde hair falling into his eye as he did so.

"And if it doesn't work out . . . um . . . we go our separate ways and no hard feelings, right?"

"Uh-huh."

I stared at my feet. The voice in my head working at breakneck speed. *Willow . . . you're not . . . Willow . . . Oh, Jesus Christ you . . .*

I looked up at him.

"OK. Let's give this thing a go."

Patrick swooped in and hugged me, squeezing the breath out of me. He placed his hands on either side of my face and swept down to kiss me. His soft, pillowy lips pressed into mine as I reciprocated. He pulled away and looked at his watch.

"Twenty-four hours starting from now." He took my hand and pulled me towards the exit doors.

"Where are we going?" I stumbled as I pulled my cabin baggage behind me.

"You'll see."

CHAPTER EIGHT

Repeating Lessons

I got back in the Hilux and clipped my seat belt as Dionne Warwick belted out the lyrics to "Walk On By."

A whirl of thoughts sped through my mind. I had made this mistake once before . . . with Rick. And now here I was acting on impulse once again, this time with Pat--but this was different, right?

What the hell have you done, Willow? Do you never learn from past mistakes?

The voice in my head wouldn't stop talking.

Now you're running off with a Californian dude. You don't know anything about him.

"Oh shut up!" I said to myself.

I glanced over at Pat as he drove down the freeway out of San Francisco towards Half Moon Bay. For a brief second, we locked eyes and smiled.

"You know they lock people up for talking to themselves!" he laughed.

I guessed he was just as nervous as me.

"Where are we going?" I asked looking out the window.

"You'll see in a minute or two once we get around this bend."

I clutched onto my Kate Spade handbag. It was getting dark. I was struck by pangs of regret.

"What will my boss say when she finds out I didn't board that flight?" I said.

"Relax!" Pat drew me a sideways look. "I'll buy you a new ticket. Just lie low, tell her you have a cold and you're switching your phone off for

24 hours." Pat drew me a wicked glance. "You're allowed a day off, Willow."

"I know, I know. It's just that I'm at her beck and call 24 hours a day, and I don't anticipate it changing any day soon." I stared out of the window, lost in thought. "Not with these other boutiques that are waiting to be launched."

Pat placed his hand on my knee. "Can you just chill for a moment?" He gave me another sideways look, shaking his head, "Park the work stuff?"

I bit my lip.

Patrick changed the subject. "Look at the awesome views! I know it's misty but you can just about make out the Pacific Coastline," he said. "You want to go surfing with me at sunrise?"

"Surfing! You surf? Oh! Now that makes a lot of sense . . ."

"What do you mean?" he looked confused.

"The hair." I said in a matter-of-fact tone. Pat raised an eyebrow but kept his eyes on the road.

I went on. "I noticed your hair is sometimes slicked back and other times . . ." I paused and stared at him.

"Go on . . ." he encouraged.

"It's just that . . . um . . . sometimes you look like you've been dragged through a hedge backwards."

The moment the words escaped my mouth, I regretted saying them.

"Cheeky!" he grinned taking no offence. Pat ran a hand through his floppy quaff and glanced at his reflection in the rear-view mirror. "I guess you're right. Seawater plays havoc with the hair."

"I . . . er . . . I kinda like it," I said shyly. Pat smiled at me. We drove on in silence.

"So where are we going to stay?" I asked excitedly.

Pat took a turn off the freeway onto a town road. "You'll see in a couple of minutes," he said.

A few moments later, we pulled into the gravel driveway of the estate belonging to Brodie's Winery. Pat opened the door for me and helped me step down from the Hilux.

A woman in her late 50s dressed in a black and white housekeeper's uniform came out from the gorgeous Mediterranean stone-clad house and offered to help with my luggage.

"Willow. This is Kate." he said.

I shook hands with Kate.

"Pleased to meet you, dear." Kate locked eyes with Pat and gave him a wry look. "We didn't get much notice of your arrival."

Pat took my hand as we stepped inside the house. I was nervous as hell as I clutched onto him.

Surely he's not taking me to meet the parents? We haven't even dated!

He must have read my thoughts. "Don't worry. Mom and dad are on a business trip."

I looked up at him and shook my head. "Thank God for that! Way too soon to be meeting the parents."

I took a deep breath and stepped inside the main house. The interior of the great room was decked out like a luxurious Swiss chalet. The room consisted of a vaulted ceiling with old worn beams taking centre stage. A huge crystal chandelier hung from the ceiling, casting a warm, ambient glow over the whole room, as a log fire roared in the grate.

Kate appeared from the kitchen and beckoned me to give her my jacket.

"So, you were on your way back to New York?" she asked, carefully folding my jacket over her arm.

"Yes. I was supposed to fly back to New York today but Patrick here, persuaded me to stay for another day." I turned to look at him. He locked eyes with me and smiled.

"I'm glad you decided to stay another night, dear. The beauty business is fast-paced, it'll be nice for you to have some to relax," she said.

We all stood in a circle in the great room. I didn't know what to say or do next.

Kate took control. "OK, come with me and I'll show you to the guest quarters."

She motioned for me to follow her down the hall.

"Dinner will be ready in half an hour, you'll have time to get settled in."

"Thank you, Kate."

She glanced over at Patrick. "Will you go to the cellar and pick out the award-winning 1977 for Willow, please?"

Pat leaned over and hugged me. "Will do."

I followed Kate out of the house and back towards where we had parked up.

"The guest quarters are just in here, dear." Motioned the housekeeper, as she pointed towards a tiny, whitewashed cottage. She took out a large silver key from her starched white apron pocket.

"Will I have this all to myself?" I asked, in awe of the hospitality I was receiving.

"Of course! We don't have anyone else staying with us until next week." She put the key in the door and opened it to reveal a homely, shabby chic interior.

A sparkling chandelier, similar to the one in the main house, caught my attention as it lit up the interior of the small living room. The living room featured two miniature chesterfield sofas placed opposite each other over a carved driftwood coffee table. A chic display comprised of a pile of glossy interior design magazines and a tray filled with crystal glasses and decanters of whisky and brandy took centre stage.

"We'll see you at 7:00 pm back in the dining room." She smiled. "If you need anything at all, just press '0' and call through to me."

I nodded and closed the door behind her. Adjacent to the living room was a good-sized bedroom. I threw myself down on the pale blue broderie Anglaise linens. As I lay on top of the bed, I scanned the room and noted the delicate china blue fleur de lys wallpaper that looked like it had been bought from a Parisian flea market.

"What bloody great taste!"

In the corner of the room stood and old Shaker-styled wardrobe with wicker basket on the top filled with plump pillows and tartan blankets.

On the bedside tables, pretty lamps with wrought iron bases cast a warm glow throughout the space.

The large and comfortable bed was encased in an ornate bedstead which was gilded in gold paint. There were chips in the paintwork but this only added to the effect. I got up and walked into the bathroom.

A swoon-worthy claw-foot porcelain tub took pride of place under a window that looked onto the rows and rows of vines.

The window was open and a pretty lace curtain flickered in the sea breeze. I could hear the Pacific Ocean waves crash against the rocks below. The whole effect was mesmerising.

I poured myself a large goblet of brandy from the decanter and strolled around the cottage, drinking in the atmosphere. The liquid warmed my belly and brought a smile to my face.

Oh how utterly blissful it must be to live here.

On the wall behind me, there was a line of framed certificates awarded to the winery. They were all dated from the last five years and I noticed that the family had been awarded a gold star for their signature Brodie's wine.

"No bloody wonder! It's gorgeous!"

Then the thought struck me. *The barman I had looked down my nose at in San Francisco lives here! How wrong I had been about him.*

I unzipped my trolley bag and searched for a fresh outfit to wear for dinner. Thankfully I had the foresight before I left New York to pack one summery dress--a pink, floaty number that was in stark contrast to my minuscule widow's wardrobe that allowed me to get dressed in a New York minute.

The brandy was working a treat, helping me to feel more relaxed. I looked at my watch and thought about the flight I should have been on. Once again, I felt slightly nervous at bunking off for the day.

You deserve some happiness after all the hard work you've put out said the little voice of reason in my head.

I undressed and stepped into the huge walk-in shower, promising myself that I could laze in the luxurious tub in the morning. Standing under the invigorating rainfall shower, it dawned on me that I hadn't shaved my legs or done a self-tan in months.

I tensed up at thought of my delicate pink dress. I stared at my legs.

"Oh no." I gasped.

A pink summer dress against hairy, milk-blue legs is just not going to cut it.

But I was stuck. I had only brought one dress and I didn't imagine there would be a local store where I could purchase a pair of tights. I stepped out of the shower, wrapped a huge white towel around me and rummaged through the cupboard for supplies of self-tanner.

"Please God! There has to be a bottle in here somewhere."

Bingo! I found one. It was in a branded bottle that I didn't recognize.

Must be a local Californian brand.

I dried myself then sat down on the leopard print stool and prepared to apply the self-tanner. But I couldn't find applicators or gloves.

Nothing else for it! Here goes!

Half-way through the application process, the results were catastrophic. My legs burned and itched like hell. I studied the box's small print and discovered I was applying an old brown hair dye to my legs.

I jumped back into the shower and rinsed the horrible unguent off my legs, splashing brown hair dye everywhere. My legs stung from the bleach as I yelled.

There was a knock at the door.

"Who is it?" I called through, wrapping myself once again in the large white towel, which was now splashed and splattered in filthy brown hair dye stains.

"It's me. Pat. Are you OK in there?"

Shit!

"I heard some noises. Thought I'd best check in on you!"

I scrambled around on the wet, stained floor, with makeup streaking down my face. I knew I was in need of assistance. There was nothing else for it. I opened the door.

He peered in, staring first at me then over my shoulder at the mess behind me.

"Holy Fuck! What the hell are you doing? I only left you alone ten minutes ago."

I stepped in pain from one bare foot to the other. He looked down at my stained legs.

"What have you done?"

I picked up the almost empty container and showed him it.

"I thought I was using self-tanner." I looked down then up at him. "My legs were too white for my pink dress."

I sensed Pat taking everything in at once.

"You? In a pink dress?" He began to laugh.

I was insulted.

"And what's wrong with me in a pink dress?" I said.

"I only ever seen you in black. Or your 'fake airline' uniform." He was mocking me now.

Cheeky git!

"Come on, come with me. I'll take you to Kate, she'll know what to do."

I pulled the white, stained towel around me, while Pat held out a white-towelling dressing gown for me to wear. I shivered as he led the way across the courtyard into the main house.

Pat was laughing. I had never seen him laugh so hard.

"Shut up! It's not funny!" I snapped as the lotion continued to scratch and burn the skin on my legs. But even I could see how silly I must have looked and began to giggle.

"Thank God your parents are away. Imagine they got to meet me looking like this."

Pat nodded then passed me over to Kate, leaving me in an acute state of embarrassment.

"Never mind lovely, happens to the best of us," she clucked.

Oh well . . . guess I'm the entertainment for the night.

Kate gave me a clean, large white towel from the storeroom and handed me a pair of slippers.

"I'm ever so sorry! This is all my fault. I should have emptied the old supplies out of the cottage before you arrived!" Kate narrowed her eyes. "Pat didn't give us much notice of your arrival. Just glad that Viv's not here. That's his mom. She wouldn't be impressed, I can tell you that."

Kate cleansed the skin and dabbed some calamine lotion on my legs, soothing the burning sensation. I was grateful for her kindness.

"I'll make you some coffee, dearie. I think you've had quite a day."

Does she smell the alcohol on my breath? Oh no!

She handed me a small white cotton bag emblazoned with winery's logo. "Take this. Just some supplies to tide you over."

I peeked inside and spotted a toothbrush sealed in cellophane, a tiny bottle of mouth-wash, a box of Tylenol and a package of make-up remover wipes.

"We often have visitors staying over, so we give out these little amenity bags."

"Thanks so much, Kate."

I was beginning to feel more comfortable sitting there in her storeroom as she set about her housekeeping tasks.

Twenty minutes later, she appeared back in the room.

"That's the table set for dinner."

My hint for me to move.

"How much time do I have?"

She checked the time. "Ten minutes."

I left the storeroom feeling vaguely like a naughty schoolgirl. I made my way back across the courtyard towards the cottage. I dreaded going back into the bathroom and seeing the chaos that awaited me. I opened the door and peeked in. The bathroom looked like nothing had happened. It had been returned to its pristine state.

"Kate," I mumbled under my breath. "I owe you one."

***

Dinner with Patrick Brodie was an entertaining experience. He was animated and in great spirits.

Inevitably the conversation turned to the pop-up stores.

Pat listened hard as I spoke of the trials and tribulations that Mrs. G. had gone through.

"So, she did jail time?" he inquired, raising one eyebrow, "For harbouring illegal immigrants?"

"Yes. She did. She did her time and paid for her crime." I stared back at him, intent on backing up my boss. Ready to defend her to the hilt. I guessed that Pat sensed I had strong feelings on the subject.

He took a swig of the award-winning 1977 vintage red wine, holding my gaze as he drank.

"Your boss sounds like she's quite something." He smiled. I felt myself relax.

"She is." I nodded in agreement.

"A bit like yourself," he said.

I blushed, not sure of where to go next with the conversation.

Patrick clasped his hands together and stared in my direction. "I think you will make a success of everything you do." His green eyes glittered as he spoke.

"Oh? And what makes you so certain?" I asked, intrigued by his apparent belief in me.

"If you trust, it will be." He stated, then went back to eating.

I understood the language he was speaking. It was the language of the 'Laws of Attraction.'

That sentence is straight out of my yellow book.

I shook my head.

I placed my knife and fork down. "You know, Patrick . . ." I started.

"It's Pat," he chided, drawing me a wry look.

"OK . . . *Pat!*" I emphasized his name. "You know I would have listened to you a few years ago, but that stuff is so passe . . . had its day in the sun."

Pat placed his knife and fork down and stopped eating. "Really? Is that so? How come you're so jaded?"

I took a gulp of red wine, even though the voice in my head was almost screaming at me to drink coffee instead. I shrugged my shoulders. "A lot has happened to me since arriving in New York."

"Can't all be bad? Surely?"

"Well . . . there's the impending divorce to Rick." I started, looking up to gauge his reaction.

"People get divorced all the time. It's hardly the end of the world." He declared, a self-satisfied expression took hold of his features.

I sensed his view of the world was wildly different from mine. I decided to use the age-old introvert's trick of turning the conversation around to make it all about him.

"What about you?" I looked around. "How does a bartender from San Francisco get to live in a place like this?"

Willow, reign it in, you're beginning to sound like a pain in the ass.

But I felt slighted in that he should take my apparent heartache so lightly.

Sensing my discomfort, he placed the hot palm of his hand on top of my hand, "You just need to stay positive . . . make things happen." He smiled.

"Easy for you to say when you live in a place like this," I said.

Now you sound like a child.

"We come from humble beginnings, Willow. This whole estate was built one stone boulder at a time. My parents never gave up hope. Even when the bank attempted to bankrupt them by calling in the loan."

That revelation shocked me.

"Really? What happened in the end?"

Pat sat back in his chair and stalled for a minute, "Well, the community of Half Moon Bay learned of their plight and got together to buy shares in the estate."

"Wait . . . what? So, you guys are like the tenants of the estate?" I asked. I was shocked. I had assumed they had inherited wealth.

"We were at the beginning, until year by year they built the trade up and the income started to flow in." His eyes crinkled with the memory. "Then they reached the stage where they were able to buy more shares in the estate until they owned it outright." He devoured the contents of his plate. "That only just happened a few years back," he said.

I felt humbled in his company. "I suppose I just assumed that you guys were mega-wealthy . . ." I shook my head, staring at Pat as he continued to eat, "Your family and community sound incredible."

He leaned over and whispered, "You're not so bad yourself."

Kate entered the room and began to clear away the dinner plates. I took the opportunity to excuse myself. "Where's the bathroom?"

"Just down the hall on the right-hand side." Kate replied.

I made my way out of the dining room and headed in the direction of the hallway. I needed a moment to myself, to digest the information I had just heard. I closed the door behind me and stared at myself in the mirror. I was a mess.

What the hell does he see in me?

The pink dress looked awful on me, the rushed makeup was a disaster. Mixing drinks didn't help things either. My legs were still stinging from my earlier futile attempts at self-tan.

I splashed my wrists with cold water, smoothed my hair down and checked my teeth for signs of red lipstick. I had lots of flecks of lipstick on my teeth.

Get it together, Willow.

I hurriedly removed the offending speckles with my fingertip of my right index finger, shrugged my shoulders back and stood up straight.

That's better.

I walked out of the bathroom and headed back to the dining room where Pat and Kate were deep in conversation about Coco and the latest wine launch.

There's that name again. Who the hell is Coco?

Patrick looked up as I walked back in. He looked concerned for me. "You OK? You look tired."

I nodded my head. "I am tired. I think I best go to bed." Kate caught my gaze. "It's been a long couple of days."

Bed? I just want to spend time with Pat . . . alone!

Patrick took the hint. He pushed his chair back and moved in my direction. "I'll walk her back to the cottage," he told Kate.

"Thank you for dinner. It was exceptional." I smiled at Kate.

"Good night, Willow."

Once outside and out of earshot, I whispered, "Your set-up here is something else . . ." I scanned the surroundings of the winery, "You are so lucky to live here."

"You're right." He exhaled, taking a breath of the chilled night air. "I am very lucky." He clutched my hand tightly and led me towards the cottage door."

"Your parents are something else, to build this place from scratch."

Patrick nodded in agreement. "They are, aren't they? They've been my inspiration since I was this high."

He placed his hand adjacent to his knee. "When I was just a wee laddie," He mocked in a slurred Scottish accent.

I play slapped him on the shoulder, then he put his arm around me as we ambled back towards the cottage.

It was dark outside in the courtyard. The moon was glistening off the ocean and the breeze had whipped up a bit, bringing a welcome coolness to the air. The cicadas buzzed in the vineyard as the fragrance of night jasmine flitted through my nostrils.

I leaned against the cottage wall and let out a huge sigh. "You're just so lucky to live here," I gasped, intoxicated with the warmth of the wine and heady fragrance of the jasmine, while butterflies did back-flips in my belly.

I noticed him glance at me, but he said nothing. He looked like he was going to say something then thought better of it.

"It's not all vineyard chic you know . . . I spend half the week sleeping in a bunk in the back of the bar."

This was a light bulb moment for me.

"So that's why you can go from looking scruffy as hell to looking like you just walked out of the pages of a glossy magazine."

Patrick furrowed his brows.

Oops! Maybe I went too far.

Patrick checked me up and down, smiling, "Um . . . you're the one to talk!"

I laughed. "Yep. Time for me to be out of this horrible dress."

"I can help you with that," he said.

"Thanks for walking me back, Patrick. I mean Pat." I went in behind the cottage door and began to close it shut. But Pat had other ideas.

"Do you want to walk down to the beach with me?" He pulled two silver flasks out of his chino pockets.

"I nabbed some of the '77," he smiled.

"Are you for real? The award-winning wine?"

"I know. That's why I took it." His expression was full of mirth as he stared at me.

I bit my lip.

"Come on! You've got to live a little."

"OK." I answered, unconvinced. "But give me a few minutes to get changed out of this horrible dress."

"I can stay if you want." He stepped in closer. "And help you get out of that."

"Cheeky!" I pushed him towards the doorway and closed the door behind him.

Ten minutes later, I emerged to find him sitting on the gravel, smoking a cigarette and drinking from the flask.

"I didn't know you smoked?" I was shocked. "How can you surf and be a smoker?

"There's a lot you don't know about me." He reached out his hand and pulled me towards him. He scanned me up and down. "And anyways, I only smoke when I drink." He checked me up and down again. "I have to say I prefer you in this." He pointed to my scuffed trainers and jeans, "it's way more becoming."

I pulled the over-sized sweater down over my knees. It was black and misshapen and there were threads hanging from the sleeve.

"I've never seen you so unkempt . . . but I think I like it!"

He leaned in for a kiss before pulling me in the direction of the ocean.

"Come on . . . this way."

The stars twinkled in the dark skies above as we lay on the damp sand, cuddling, drinking and smoking, listening to the hypnotic sounds of the waves crash ashore against the rocks. We had the beach to ourselves.

"Just think. If you had said 'no', you would be in flight right now." He stared deep into my eyes. "But I'm glad you said 'yes'." He pulled me tight towards him and I could feel my heart pounding in my chest.

I lay there with my eyes closed, inhaling his musky scent, engraving this scene on my memory, hoping it would never fade. When I peeked my eyes open, I noticed that Pat's eyelids were firmly shut. I could tell he was holding onto this memory just as much as me.

Eventually, I spoke up. "So . . ." I sighed, as I struck up the courage to ask him about his life. "You know a lot about me . . . what about you?

Patrick lay back on the sand, drew on his cigarette and blew a smoke ring.

"Nothing much to tell." He looked up at me with those sea-green eyes of his, his hair melding into the sand.

That's not good enough. I want more. Way more!

I scooped up a handful of sand grains and let them drain through my fingertips as I stared across at the Pacific Ocean. One by one, I picked up some smooth white pebbles and made them into a little pile on top of the sand.

I felt safe in his company. Safe in a way I never experienced with Rick or Jake for that matter.

"Go on . . . tell me something." I pleaded. "I want to know all about you!"

Pat sat up halfway, placed his weight on his elbows as he stared out to the ocean.

He took a long drag on his cigarette and turned to look at me. "I have a little daughter. Coco. She's six." He gauged my reaction.

"Wait!" My mind flitted back to the day I thought I saw him on the street. "So that *was* you? I thought I saw you outside the coffee house holding hands with a little blonde girl. I came out to look for you, but you were gone."

"Mid-week? She was wearing a school blazer?" Pat took another drag on his cigarette. "Yep, that would have been me on the school run."

"Wow. So, you're a dad." I wasn't quite sure how to feel about that news. If truth be told I felt . . . *whiplashed*. "I never had you down as a dad."

Pat cocked his head to the side and shrugged.

"I'm 39 years old, Willow. I've had a life."

Now I felt stupid. "Of course. Yes, of course you've had a life."

I was dying to ask him about Coco's mum but couldn't quite bring myself to ask.

Pat let out a huge sigh. I wasn't quite sure if it was one of relief or regret.

He lay his head down on my lap, with his hands dug deep into his pockets and stared up at me.

"I guess you're probably wondering who her mom was?" he said.

I shrugged. I didn't want to say 'yes' and I didn't want to say 'no.' but Pat carried on regardless.

"Coco's mom passed away in childbirth." Pat closed his eyes. It had taken all his strength to tell me.

I cupped my hands around his chin and stared down at him.

"Oh my God. You poor souls." I saw a solitary tear travel down Pat's cheek as he kept his eyes shut tight. His chin quivered as the depth of his grief got the better of him. I felt like I wanted to cry with him.

"You're the first lady I've asked out since then," he said.

Ten minutes . . . maybe twenty passed in silence as the clouds outlined by moonlight sped across the sky.

Pat looked at his watch. "It's getting late."

"Shame."

He pulled me up, "C'mon, got to get you back. I'm surfing in a few hours from now. You can join me, but you might prefer to stay in bed.

We ambled back up the hill towards the winery, hand in hand. Outside the door to the cottage, I once again leaned against the stone wall and stared at him.

"Thanks for a lovely evening."

I opened the door to let myself in.

"So." He paused. "You're not inviting me in for coffee?"

"Nope." I giggled.

"You're a tease, Willow Campbell.

I checked my watch.

"At this moment in time, I'm still legally married," I said.

His expression fell. "How long for?"

I tilted my head looking skywards. "Three more weeks."

He pulled me in close, kissing me as I closed my eyes.

"Goodnight, Miss Campbell."

"Goodnight, Mr. Brodie."

***

I closed the door behind me and leaned against the wall, staring at my surroundings. My head spun with giddy excitement. I rolled the white pebbles between the palms of my hands as I went over everything he had told me. He had taken me completely by surprise.

"Patrick Brodie is a single dad," I said out loud.

In normal circumstances, I would have got on the phone to Jackson and mulled this latest turn of events with him, but I didn't know how to reach him. I threw myself down on the elegant sofa and poured myself another brandy.

He's so right. The fact he has a daughter means he has likely led a full life but how tragic to lose his wife in this way . . . but do I want to get involved with a man who already has a child?

That single thought cut through the brandy vapours and sobered me up in an instant, while the voice in my head kicked into high gear.

Best you end this now before anyone gets hurt.

But I really like him, in fact I think I'm falling for him.

"Oh bloody hell!" I stood up and poured the remainder of the contents of the glass down the sink. I walked into the bathroom and turned the shower on, while I rummaged in my luggage for something that might resemble a nightdress.

As I stood under the hot running water, my mind flipped back and forwards. I knew I was getting away ahead of myself but I couldn't help it . . . *Businesswoman or step-mother to someone else's child?*

I stepped out the shower, dried myself and pulled on a nightie that was destined for the washing machine, then pulled back the sumptuous duvet and crawled into bed. Sleep did not arrive until the early hours of the morning.

At 5:00 am, I awoke with a pounding headache. My tongue felt like sandpaper as I swore off alcohol for good (yet again). The memories from the night before came in at breakneck speed as my legs began to smart.

I needed more calamine lotion and an aspirin. I turned over in the bed and rummaged inside the little amenities bag that Kate had given me the night before.

Oh, thank God! Everything that I need. Kate you are a doll.

Then I remembered how I had insulted Patrick about his shabby appearance.

My God, the guy works so hard, takes care of his daughter . . . never blinkin' stops and here I am giving him a hard time.

Just then, I heard the soft crunch of footsteps out on the gravel courtyard. The sun was only beginning to rise.

Curiosity got the better of me, I climbed out of bed and peeked through the curtains. I recognized the silhouette placing a surfboard on top of the Hilux. It belonged to Patrick.

Where's he off to?

I recalled our conversation on the beach.

I pulled on the dressing gown that was hanging on the back of the bedroom door and picked up the slippers that Kate have given me. I stepped out onto the gravel courtyard, the stones crunching under my feet, as I walked.

"Patrick," I whispered. He turned around and stared at me.

"Hey beautiful . . . what are you doing up at this time in the morning?" he asked, his arms were outstretched.

I walked towards him and hugged him while he mussed up my bed-head hair. "Loving this au natural look. I didn't know you had freckles," he said.

I stared up at him, "You woke me up!"

Patrick laughed softly as he pulled me in tight towards him, "I'm going surfing, I thought you'd want to sleep on, so I didn't bother to knock on your door." He leaned in for a kiss. "You want to join me?"

It was chilly and misty, standing there in the dim light of dawn. I hugged myself as I shivered.

"I don't know the first thing about surfing. I'm a city girl--didn't you notice?"

He carried on strapping the surfboard to the rack, then checked the time.

"Come with me. You can sit on the beach, but you'll need to hurry . . . go and put something warm on."

"OK, give me a minute." I rushed back to the cottage and threw on my running gear--not that I ever went running. I grabbed a warm jumper, pulled on my trainers and re-joined Patrick in the Hilux.

"So where are we going?" I asked. It was so rare for me to be awake at this time in the morning.

Patrick drove the wagon out of the courtyard and revved the engine as we pulled up onto the highway.

"We're going to Mavericks Beach. Home to the biggest surf on the West Coast."

"Oh cool!" I had never heard of Mavericks Beach or Half Moon Bay for that matter.

"At this time of the year, we have the biggest waves, you'll see for your-self in a minute or two."

I settled into the passenger seat and drank in the views as the mist be-gan to clear. The road was almost empty.

"Can we put on some music?" I pressed a few buttons on the music system and Hope Sandoval sang the emotive lyrics to *Fade Into You* by Mazzy Star.

I sang along as I watched the waves in the Pacific Ocean crash ashore onto the rocks below.

Now wasn't the time to ask questions about Coco or his wife or any other aspect of his life. I guessed this little magical corner of the world was starting to get under my skin and I wanted to savour every minute.

Hope stopped singing and the adverts came on. "You're so lucky to live here," I sighed. Patrick glanced at me but said nothing. I guessed he was trying to figure out what to say to me about last night. We pulled into the parking lot and I watched as he got his surfboard and belongings ready. It was cold, the wind was whipping up and the crazy waves appeared to be getting wilder by the minute.

He pulled a canvas foldable chair and a couple of blankets from the back of the Hilux and walked me to the beach, where he assembled everything.

"Sit here. I won't stay out long . . . promise."

I was about to say, "OK," but he was gone, running off to join the other surfers.

I tried to keep my eye on him but it became impossible, and he was lost among the throng of surfers. I held my breath each time a huge wave swelled up then crashed ashore with a myriad of surfers riding the waves.

I gripped my knees in anticipation. "How the hell do they do that?"

I couldn't say it was enjoyable being an observer on the beach. I was too concerned about his safety and wanted it to be over. My nerves couldn't take it. I looked around me and noticed a few others dotted around on the beach, but they didn't appear to have a concern in the world.

Chill out Willow. He's been surfing since he was a kid. He knows what he's doing. You have absolutely nothing to worry about and perhaps you shouldn't care so much so soon.

The trouble was, I did care.

***

I dug my bare feet into the cool, golden sand of Maverick's Beach and reflected on my own life: There I was running about here, there, and everywhere, sorting out other peoples' problems. It had been so long since I had been on the tools. My makeup brushes were largely untouched. Since Gigi had re-hired me, my life had become a whirlwind, while my work-life balance was zilch. I even felt guilty for sneaking a day off to spend with Patrick.

I made a promise to myself: One day I will return to this beach.

Patrick re-appeared with a couple of his pals.

"Willow!" he called. "This is Leo . . . and this is Jim."

I stood up and shook their hands. They were freezing cold standing in their wet suits, their longish hair pushed back behind their ears. I sensed they were full of vitality and abuzz with adrenalin.

"Well?" Patrick asked, "Did you see us ride that gigantic wave?"

"I did!" I lied. "You guys were amazing."

"Right! Let's go!" He said. "Got to get you ready to go back to the city."

On the short journey back to Brodie's Winery, I had so many questions about Pat's life-his surfing habit, his day-to-day life and, most importantly, his little daughter, Coco.

"Is this how you start your day? Every day?" I asked.

"Yep. It's like an addiction." He chuckled to himself. "Been doing it since I was eight."

My mouth hung open. "How long can you keep surfing for? Is there an age limit?"

Patrick laughed. "You're only as old as you feel," he said. "But there's no age limit. You should try it sometime . . . you might enjoy it."

"I guess so."

We pulled into the parking lot and Patrick checked the time. "Right.

We've got forty-five minutes before we have to leave again. I'll go and get changed into my work gear." He turned and pecked me on the cheek. "I'll be working in the bar tonight after I drop you at the airport." He ruffled his cold hand through my hair. "Hungry?"

"Starving!" I said.

"Help yourself to whatever Kate's laid out on the kitchen table, then I'll see you back here at 9:00 o'clock."

I looked on as Pat dashed off to the family home to get changed.

Back in the guest cottage, I contemplated running the bath but soon realized I would have no time to enjoy it, so I stepped into the shower and washed off the last few patches of Calamine lotion that were stuck to my legs. I searched my trolley bag for another potential outfit but was resigned to putting on the same thing I had worn the previous night.

I hope he doesn't notice. Of course he's going to notice. I should have brought more clothes with me, dammit.

I opened my makeup bag and set to work. I had no idea what Pat had lined up for us up in San Francisco. He kept telling me that everything was to be a surprise. I don't remember going out with anyone who had put so much time and effort into dating me . . . like, ever.

I set to work and applied my makeup, sweeping a fine eyeliner on the top lid followed by two layers of mascara. Then I applied two coats of my current favourite Chanel Pirate lipstick. The Californian sunshine had brought out my freckles which were scattered all over my cheeks. Happy with my artistic work, I spritzed my outfit with the Plane Jane signature fragrance then checked myself in the mirror.

The butterflies in my belly sprung into life as I anticipated our final few hours together.

Will he introduce me to his daughter? I knew she went to school in the city and returned home to Half Moon Bay on the weekends. His mother and Coco live in a condo during the school week so that Pat could see his daughter as much as possible while he ran the bar. The arrangement seemed to fit all members of the family. Pat told me that his mum, Vivian, ran her other businesses from the city when Coco was in school. I guessed that Vivian had taken over the motherly duties when Pat's wife passed away.

I pulled on my runners and set off towards the kitchen, trailing my trolley bag over the white gravel.

"Did he not help you with your luggage?" Kate tutted, shaking her head as she stood at the doorway to the main house.

"Och . . . it's fine. I'm used to doing everything myself." I smiled at Kate as she plied me with plates filled with tasty scones and jam, croissants and a platter of smoked meats and Swiss cheeses.

"Did you have a nice evening? I hope you got some rest?" she eyed me with a mischievous look.

"I did. Thank you." I looked around while I endured the interrogation from Kate. "I ended up going to the beach with Pat."

"That man and his surfing." She tutted again. "What're your hobbies?"

I was stumped. *Me? Hobbies?*

"Oh . . . em. Well." I had nothing to give.

Kate searched my face for a few seconds.

"Anything?"

"I like to read books." I lied.

No, you don't. You haven't picked up a book in years. The only book you've paid attention to was the infamous 'yellow book' and look where that got you.

"Oh! And I like to cook." I was pleased with my quick thinking. I hadn't cooked a dinner in weeks, preferring the ease of takeout.

Kate stared at me a moment too long for comfort. "Mmmm." She mumbled.

I guessed she could see through my little white lies, but her questions got me thinking. *What do I really do with my time?*

Kate's questions shone a light on my empty life. Lately, all I seemed to do was work.

My spirits sank.

"I have no idea what you Scots like to eat for breakfast, so I made a variety of dishes: oatmeal, continental meats and cheeses and some of my delicious pains au chocolat direct from the bakery up the road." She beamed proudly, standing in front of her fare.

"I can't remember the last time I had a bowl of porridge for breakfast." The aroma triggered a memory from childhood, standing in my mum's warm kitchen on a freezing winter's morning waiting on the school socks warming up inside the big oven.

"Mmm . . . this tastes delicious."

Then I wrapped one of the Pain Au Chocolat in a napkin. "I'll take this with me for the journey, in case I feel hungry later."

"Uh huh . . . I'm guessing the sea air has given you a good appetite." She cocked an eyebrow and winked at me.

I couldn't wait to get away. It was as if she could see straight through me and was able to read my thoughts at the same time.

"What time's your flight back?"

"Pat booked me on the 2:15 pm. Should arrive home around 10ish eastern time. Then it's straight back to work tomorrow."

"You New Yorkers!" she shook her head. "You need to take your feet off the gas and slow down a bit.

I'm only 34 . . . for Chrissakes . . . what does she want me to do? Retire.

"Don't worry, I'll fall asleep on the flight home." I gave her my best attempt at a gracious smile as Pat revved the engine.

"Sounds like someone's impatient to leave." Kate clucked. "You better be going."

I nodded and gathered up my belongings as I headed for the door.

"Thanks for your hospitality, Kate. I had a great time and I enjoyed getting to know you all." I held out my hand to shake hers. Kate's grip was tight.

A concerned expression stretched across her face.

"Where's he taking you?"

"No idea! I guess it's a secret," I shrugged.

"You know he hasn't gone out with anyone since Natalie passed away?"

Kate's eyes bore through me, as if she was trying to make up her mind whether or not she thought I was 'up to the job' of taking on Patrick.

"Yes. He told me last night." Her questioning had got my back up.

Kate looked relieved. "It's just been such a terrible time . . . frankly, I don't know how he's managed to soldier on without her."

"I guess Coco got him through?" I offered.

"So, he told you about his daughter?" She looked relieved.

"Yes. Told me all about her last night . . ." I could feel my face redden with discomfort as I second-guessed the next question.

Kate lurched straight in. "What about you? You got any kids?"

"No." I stared back at her daring her to ask me another question. She was really starting to annoy me now.

What bloody business is it of hers anyway?

"No." She folded the towel and placed it on top of the marble bar. "I didn't think you would have."

"And you're absolutely right." Kate returned to loading the dishwasher. "That little girl saved him. If it wasn't for her . . . well . . . I'm not so sure that Pat would be with us today."

Holy Fuck. She's not beating about the bush.

I guessed she was being protective of him, didn't want him getting hurt again.

I wanted to run away. Kate picked up on my vibes and ushered me towards the door.

"You have a great time up in San Francisco." She beamed holding the kitchen door open for me. "Hopefully we'll see you again soon." Her expression told me that she didn't expect she would see me again ever.

I walked out onto the gravel courtyard, my mind whirring with the names Natalie and Coco.

Dusty Springfield sang the *Look of Love* as we drove back up to San Francisco. So far the time I had spent with Pat had been unforgettable.

"What's the matter? You seem miles away." He asked, a concerned look had crept across his face.

I attempted to brighten up. "It's nothing!" I shrugged, "just taking in all the sights and sounds." I proffered a fake smile but I guessed he could see straight through me.

"Has . . . um . . . Kate been speaking to you? About me?" He looked concerned now.

I knew I had to be straight with him.

"Yes."

He blew air out of his mouth as he tutted and shook his head. I felt bad for him.

"It's OK, Pat." I placed my hand on his knee as he drove. I didn't know what else to say.

He sighed loudly.

"I'm actually in awe of you and how you've soldiered through." I offered him an encouraging smile. "A lot of men would have walked away and shirked their responsibilities . . . but you stayed the course. You should be proud of yourself . . . it can't have been easy."

Pat turned to look at me. "I haven't done it single-handedly. My parents stepped in."

"So when will I meet her?" I asked, determined now to be introduced to his offspring.

Patrick frowned. "Who? Coco?" He turned to look at me. "You really want to meet Coco?"

"Yes. I do." The defiance in my voice took me by surprise.

I sensed the tension dissipate from the car interior as he relaxed.

"If it's OK with you, I'll bring her with me to the Vinexpoamerica."

"Oh! OK then." I forced a smile.

Wasn't expecting that!

You've landed yourself in it now, Willow.

It was time to change the subject.

"How much time do we have left?" I asked.

Pat glanced at his watch. "Just under three hours," he said.

I looked over in the direction of the Pacific Ocean and recalled lying on the beach at midnight with Pat by my side.

"So where are we going now?" I asked, trying my best to raise my spirits.

Pat touched his nose with his finger.

"It's a secret?" I asked.

"Yep," he replied.

"Can you give me a clue at least? I mean do I need to dress up?" I only had so many outfits available in my cabin luggage and I had already used up every permutation available.

Pat shook his head. "No. You're fine as you are. Just sit back and relax."

I lay my head back and began to doze off. I hadn't been so comfortable in the presence of another man, like ever.

Thirty-five minutes later we were back in the city. Patrick parked the Hilux in the car parking lot behind Brodie's Bar then took my hand as walked down the street towards Van Ness Cable Car.

"Have you been on one of these?"

"No. I never got the chance. Too busy working."

"That's what I thought. Come on. Jump on!" He held out his hand to me and pulled me onto the trolley.

We bundled into the car and sat next to an elderly man in his mid-70s who was listening to Elvis Presley sing *An American Trilogy* on his antiquated hand-held cassette player. The words to the song always teared me up.

"What's up?" Patrick put his arms around me. "You look sad."

I bit my lip and held back a tear.

He sensed not to enquire further. Instead, he pulled me in tight.

"I'll be OK in a minute or two," I sniffed.

Patrick tightened his grip around me.

"Those lyrics get me every time," I said.

"The one about your dad?" he said.

"Yes. That one."

Patrick tightened his grip around me.

"Where are we going?" I tried to change the subject.

"Twin Peaks."

I stared out of the window at the hustle and bustle of the city streets.

"I used to watch "The Streets of San Francisco" when I was a kid. Who would have thought I would end up working here?"

Pat smiled at me then slunk down in his seat and spoke in a low voice, "I want you to see the sights . . . then maybe one day you can show me Glasgow?"

Finally . . . a guy who wants to travel!

I shook his hand.

"Deal."

At our destination, we jumped off the cable car and made our way towards a line of coaches.

"Jump on." Pat directed.

Twenty minutes later, we sat on the wall of the Twin Peaks parking lot, drinking in the unforgettable views of the city, skyscrapers sparkling in the sunlight. I saw the whole of San Francisco spread out in front of me.

"Over there you'll see Alcatraz, where they made the famous movie about the jail," he said.

"And beyond the Golden Gate Bridge is Marin County."

"Where Carmen-your cousin-lives." I giggled, laughing at myself.

As we stood there, I felt like we were becoming inseparable while all the time I was aware of the passing minutes and hours.

Patrick stared at his watch. "What do you want to do now?"

I was cold and tired.

"Can we go see a film?" I said.

"You want to catch a movie?" He looked surprised. "Of all the sights to see in San Francisco and you want to go to the movies? Strange girl." He laughed.

"Well, at least it'll be warm, and we can sit down and snuggle."

Pat caught my drift. "I know just the place." He checked his phone for screen timings. "If we hurry, we'll just be in time to catch Trainspotting at The Castro Theatre.

"Oh! I've seen it." I paused as his face fell. "But I don't mind watching it again." I didn't really care which movie was on, I just wanted to sit in a warm, dark room with Pat by my side.

"OK. Let's go."

We jumped on the tour bus that whizzed us back to the city, dropping us off just in front of the cinema.

"Looks like we got the place to ourselves." Pat winked at me as he bought two tickets from the cashier.

I don't remember much about the film, all I remember is snuggling into Pat's shoulder while holding his hand. I was aware we might look like a couple of love struck teenagers sitting in the back row, but my self-consciousness evaded me, as we snuck secret kisses in the darkness. Life was good and I didn't want the movie to end.

Later, he dropped me off at the airport car park for my flight to New York, only this time, he walked me up to the check-in bay and waited for me to collect my boarding card. I had been dreading this part of the day since I awoke earlier that morning. I turned around and faced him as I brandished my ticket in the air.

"Did you book me into First Class? I got seat 2a." I beamed.

Pat stepped in closer and pulled me in tight towards him. "It was the least I could do." He kissed my earlobe, sending shivers up my spine.

"So, what do you say, Willow Campbell? Can I see you again?" I looked up at him, losing myself in his crystal-clear emerald gaze.

"I'll check my diary and let you know." His face fell for a split-second till he realized I was joking with him. I wrapped my arms around his neck. "Of course you can."

Take it easy, Willow. Move slowly. Said the little voice. *Only fools rush in . . . remember Rick?*

"When is it?" I asked.

"When's what?" he said.

"The wine thing . . . the wine expo."

"In two weeks."

He stood in front of me, that same lock of hair falling into one eye. The collar of his denim jacket turned up at his neck, as he pulled me in close, the distinctive scent of bergamot and cedar wood enveloping me.

The previous day, I had sat at the restaurant patio envious of other loving couples saying goodbye to each other. Now it was our turn.

He ran his fingers through my hair, tucking some loose strands behind my ear.

"Are you sure you're OK with me bringing Coco?"

Pat looked hesitant, like he wasn't sure whether it was such a good idea after all.

Shit. He wants to stay with me in my apartment? Don't rush in.

I stalled. "Let's just take baby steps for the moment, you check into a hotel with your daughter and I'll come and meet you."

Pat looked crushed. "Sorry. I shouldn't have . . ."

He flushed with embarrassment. "Dammit! I'm so out of practice at this dating thing."

I began to laugh.

"It's OK." I rubbed his arm. "You know I'm just out of a relationship. I don't want to make the same mistakes twice.

I wanted all the feels of a new relationship. I didn't want a man moving in and bringing his six-year old daughter with him. I just wanted to be romanced, wined and dined and then see where things went after that.

"Now, are you really sure you're OK with me bringing Coco to New York? . . babysitters are a bit thin on the ground these days." He looked at his shoes, then up at me. "I kind of called in all my favours years ago."

Pat looked hesitant, like he wasn't sure whether or not it was such a good idea after all.

I relented.

"Bring her."

He leaned in for another kiss. This time on the lips, but I didn't complain. I could get used to those kisses.

He pulled away. "You better go now. They're calling your flight."

He stood with his hands in his pockets in the middle of the concourse and watched me walk towards the escalator. I kept turning back to wave until he was out of sight.

My smile was stretched across my face and not even a 55 minute-delay to New York could wipe it from my face.

The opening monologue to Trainspotting ran through my mind: Choose Life, Choose a Job. Choose a Career. Choose a Family. I chose Patrick Brodie.

CHAPTER NINE

Hungarian Rose

The next afternoon, I was summoned to Tallulah's Tearoom. I sensed that Mrs. G. hadn't bought my story about having a cold and staying in bed for a day.

I hope I haven't mucked up my big opportunity.

The commonsense side of my brain kicked in.

You're allowed a day off after travelling, Willow.

This made me feel a bit better about facing my boss.

For our meeting, I had chosen to wear a mint green velvet dress with a dainty bow at the waistband--very 1950s vintage. It was the norm to dress up when summoned to the tearooms and on this occasion, it felt good to be out of uniform and instead be dressed in my own clothes.

My hair was dirty from the flying and travelling but it sat better that way. One side of my hair was tucked behind my ear so that the other side swept over my face. I had spackled on my favourite Kat Von Dee foundation to hide the bags and wrinkles I was starting to develop while Elvis belted out the lyrics to *'I just can't help believing.'* I stopped in my tracks and really listened to the words that came out of the 'King's' mouth. *This time the girl is going to stay, for more than just a day.*

Could he be singing to me? Would I stay here for more than just a day?

My thoughts flitted back to Patrick and his little daughter Coco. Shivers travelled down my spine as I briefly allowed myself to think of him and I as a couple.

Could I? Could I take on this charming man and his beautiful little daughter?

Stop it, Willow.

You've only just met the guy.

My phone buzzed bringing me straight back to the here and now. It was George. He was giving me the heads up that Mrs. G. was at best displeased with me.

Blimey! He said he would cover for me.

I guessed that my boss had seen straight through his white lies after all.

I threw the phone down on top of the unmade bed.

This is all I need.

The phone buzzed again. It was Pat texting me. Telling me how much he was missing me.

My heart filled with a lovely, warm fuzzy feeling.

Bless!

I could get used to this.

This long-distance romancing wasn't so bad after all.

And I'm doing things differently this time. I'm not rushing in like a fool. I'm taking my time and enjoying every lovely minute of it.

Diana Ross was singing now. *Someday, we'll be together.* I began to dance around the small apartment. For the first time in a very long time, I felt happy. Happy to be in this new relationship, yet strangely content to be alone. I had grown since meeting Rick. I didn't need to rush in. This time I would do things differently. Of that I was sure.

I looked down at my nails. My red, shiny nails were chipped but I had made an appointment for myself at the nail bar of choice just outside my apartment in Hell's Kitchen.

Although I had enjoyed my first visit to California, and it had turned out to be an unexpected success in the romance department, I was glad to be back in my adopted home--Manhattan.

I checked the time on my vintage Kelly watch and noticed that Mrs. G. was late for our meeting.

Very unusual. Not like her at all.

As I waited, I took out the iPad and checked my emails. There were three from San Francisco. Carmen had sent over her latest sales reports and, as predicted, the new premises two doors down from Brodie's Bar had brought in an abundance of new clients, resulting in some impressive sales figures.

Perhaps the rats hadn't been so bad for business after all.

That got me thinking . . . *the rat situation had let me straight to Patrick Brodie.*

A waiter appeared in front of me as the tinkle of classical music played on in the background.

"Hi ma'am. Would you like to order now?" he asked.

I checked the time again. "I'll hold off for another few minutes, thanks."

That was when I spotted the silhouette of my boss through the revolving mercury-mirrored doorway. I noticed the door attendant assisting her with her coat. I sat upright as the butterflies in my stomach fluttered. I collected the bunch of paperwork, sorting it into a neat pile in preparation for my sales meeting. I was nervous at the thought of having bunked off for a day.

Mrs. G. walked towards the marble tables, keeping her gaze on me. I tried to guess what kind of mood she might be in. Today looked like it would be a touch of frost with the chance of thawing.

"Willow. How the devil are you?"

Smiling, I stood up and pulled her chair out for her.

"Hello, Gigi."

Dare I ask why she's late or should I just let it go? I pondered.

Just let it go, Willow.

"And how are we feeling today?" she quizzed. "George mentioned that you were feeling a tad under the weather.

Has she rumbled me?

"I'm feeling much better, thanks. And you?"

My boss's features were well-defined under a thick layer of makeup, but I noticed something different about her complexion. She was unusually pale and withdrawn. The blush sat on her cheeks in stark contrast to the pale skin underneath and the under-eye area appeared much darker than I remembered.

Perhaps the stress of launching these pop-up stores is taking its toll?

"Is everything OK?" I quizzed, noticing her hands clenched in her lap. Mrs. G. held my gaze a split-second longer than expected.

"Yes," she said. "Why do you ask?"

Her eyes were rimmed red, and she looked like she had just been crying.

"Let's begin, shall we?" Mrs. G. held out her trembling hand. "Paperwork? What do you have for me?"

I handed the sales sheets over and took the opportunity to study her gaze while she perused the figures.

I half-hoped to see a glimmer of a smile but there was nothing. Her expression was steely.

"Honestly?" she sighed as she handed the papers back to me. "I had hoped for better, Willow." She looked away from me, showcasing her disappointment.

As if someone had taken a pin to a balloon, I felt my spirits deflate.

I attempted to defend the store.

"But . . . I thought you would be pleased that we turned a profit with the launch!"

"Well, you thought wrong, dear." She pursed her lips tight. The lines around her mouth appeared more hollow.

I felt myself slip further down in my chair.

"Any profits we might have made have been eaten up with the pest extermination costs, your flights and other expenses." She pointed a long pearly-pink talon at a line on the document that was highlighted in yellow. She stared at me. "Two reservations also appear to have been made at the hotel."

I heard myself say, "I can explain that." My tone of voice was bordering on angry now.

Calm down, Willow.

From experience, I guessed there was more to come, but Mrs. G. took a sharp intake of breath before erupting into a frenzied coughing session that went on for over three minutes.

"Is everything OK?" I grabbed a linen napkin off the table and handed it to her.

"Water," she gasped.

"Bring me some water!" she covered her face with the napkin as I scrambled to get out of my seat. I got the attention of the waiter and requested a bottle of sparkling water. When I returned to our table, I stopped in my tracks, shocked. Mrs. G. appeared slumped in her chair.

"Oh my God!" I cried.

Mrs. G. waved her hand, "It's nothing. I'm fine," she said weakly.

I took another napkin off the table and dabbed her forehead, mopping up beads of sweat.

"You're anything but fine! You're soaking!"

Mrs. G. smacked my hands away and reached into her bag, pulling out a prescription note.

"Be a darling and go get this for me." She spoke in a small, exhausted voice; her coughing fit had used up a lot of her energy, leaving her drained, pale and sweaty.

The waiter brought over the bottle of water and poured her a glass. We both stood and stared while she sipped. My mind was racing.

What is the matter with her? She looks so awful!

"What are you looking at?" Mrs. G. peered up at us. "Go!" She waved her hands. "Both of you!"

I pulled on my coat and sped out of Tallulah's towards the pharmacy. I had never seen my boss look so ill and washed out.

I pulled my collar up around my neck. After the relative warmth of the tearoom, it was freezing out.

I wonder what's wrong with her?

My phone pinged. It was Pat. I texted back. I told him I would contact him later.

I stared at the paper crumpled in my hand--I was tempted to read the prescription.

No . . . That's private medical information, Willow! But . . . I wrestled with the voice in my head. I can help look after her.

I was conflicted. I hesitated then decided to read the doctor's diagnosis. PNEUMONIA.

Shit! I folded the note back up.

She needs to be at home, tucked up in bed.

I tapped the shoulder of the woman standing in front of me.

"Do you mind if I skip ahead of you? Please?" I smiled. "I've got a medical emergency."

The woman smiled back, stood aside and let me pass.

"Sure."

"Thanks so much! I really appreciate it."

"Cute accent."

It still took me by surprise when people commented on my accent. I had been in the USA long enough, but I guessed I still sounded different to most people.

There were three people in front of me. Everyone I asked to cut in front of was nice. One kid even gave me the thumbs up.

I tapped the next person waiting in line--a middle-aged man dressed in a suit.

"May I?" I assumed he had heard me tell the woman behind me.

"We're all here for medical emergencies, lady." He said, then turned his back to me.

OK, that was rude.

I bit my lip and shuffled my feet a bit before the woman behind me spoke up.

"Let her go, C'mon!"

"Move aside," said a burly man in his mid-30's. He looked like he had just stepped out of a boxing ring and had the pit stains to prove it. The suited businessman stood aside and let me go.

"Thank you." I said. "Much appreciated." I nodded at everyone in line as I stepped in front of the queue.

"Thank you."

I reached the front and handed the prescription over to the chemist. He looked at me over the top of his glasses.

"ID please."

I handed over my resident's card.

"The script is for my boss." I explained. Anxiety rose in my voice. "She's in Tallulah's--she asked me to pick this up for her."

"She should be at home, in bed." The chemist peered at me again over his glasses. I nodded in agreement as he sorted the medication into a variety of small white boxes.

"If her condition worsens, get her to hospital straight away." He pushed up his glasses. "Don't waste any time. There's a virulent strain of pneumonia doing the rounds right now. She can't take any chances."

He handed me the medication as I turned and sped off out of the pharmacy, thanking those who had helped me.

I rushed down West. 62nd Street, cursing the green velvet dress. I wished I had worn a pair of leggings with my runners instead of this ladylike nonsense.

Although stern and stoic, Mrs. G. had been my rock.

I hope she's going to be OK.

Then the thought struck me. Was her immune system weakened by her stint in prison?

I raced back into Tallulah's and rushed over to be by her side as I reiterated the chemist's recommendations.

"I am taking you home and putting you to bed!" I said sternly, it was my turn to be in charge.

Gigi Gerson looked up at me and tutted, "I'll be fine--no need to worry about me."

"But that's just the thing," I scolded, "I'm not sure that you have anyone to worry about you. Come on!" I helped her up.

Our server held out a heavy pink coat for Mrs. G. to place her arms into while the blonde hostess returned to let us know that she had hailed us a cab.

I had never been to Mrs. G.'s new apartment. I had only ever stayed in the swanky abode on West Park Avenue one Christmas night over a year ago. I had heard through the grapevine that she had lost the luxury apartment shortly after her prison stint and now was staying in a small apartment in Jackson Heights. A far cry from her previous living quarters.

Under the weight of her heavy coat, I felt her spindly, thin body lean against me as we went over the bumps in the road. I tried not to stare but her condition appeared to worsen as our journey progressed.

Her thin veneer of makeup was melting off as she ran a temperature. It was late afternoon in spring but I felt her shiver through the thickness of her coat. My mind raced.

Does she even have health insurance? Where's the nearest hospital? I can't leave her alone in this condition.

On the journey over to her apartment, I conjured up in my mind every possible scenario. On our arrival outside the apartment block, I gestured to the taxi driver to take a tip, but he sped off the moment we got out. I guessed he was off to disinfect his taxi before picking up the next passenger.

Mrs. G. was coughing into a handkerchief as I bundled her up one flight of stairs to the third door on the landing. I noticed drops of blood seep through the white handkerchief.

Be brave Willow. You can do this. Don't let her see your fear.

"Won't be long now until those antibiotics kick in . . ." I rubbed her back, placating her. "Then you'll feel so much better, I promise." I smiled, trying my best to reassure her.

She looked up at me but didn't say anything. Another bout of coughing had caught her off guard. I took off her coat and bundled her into the small bedroom. In stark contrast to the environment outside, her bedroom was a vision of designer chic. Decorated just like her office in D'Arcy's, white walls blended with the stark minimally furnished interior. Dainty linens dressed the shabby chic French-inspired King bed complete with a retro gilded rattan headboard. To complete the picture, a single vase held a single orange tulip on top of a pristine white Formica desk. A gold replica shell held a small selection of jewelry and sat on top of a small pile of expensive-looking coffee table books. A fragrance of amber and orange permeated the apartment.

This woman has such class. The kind of class that money can't buy.

I left her alone while she undressed. I went into the tiny galley kitchen and searched the cupboards for something resembling food. I found an assortment of tins, one of which was a generic brand of chicken soup.

This will do.

I turned on the gas and heated up the contents while I thought out my next move.

The pharmacist's words echoed in my head--'If there is any worsening of her condition take her straight to hospital.'

The vision of blood on the handkerchief wouldn't leave me.

I thought of all the plans she had made to launch the pop-up boutiques in a bid to earn enough money to buy D'Arcy's back again. It was a huge goal to aim for and I knew how much it meant to her that she had someone she could trust--me.

I poured the piping hot soup into a large white ceramic mug, found some bread that looked like it was two to three days beyond its sell-by date, and placed it on a saucer. Then I displayed everything on a tray and carried it into the bedroom.

Mrs. G. looked embarrassed. She grabbed a delicate beige cashmere shawl from the foot of the bed and wrapped it around herself, just as another coughing fit erupted.

"Take this." I handed her a glass of water and a pill. "It'll make you feel better." I checked her temperature with the back of my hand. Although my hand was ice-cold, she did feel hot to the touch. I was worried--the pharmacist's words played over and over in my mind.

"You can go now, dear." She waved a hand. "I'll be feeling better in the morning."

"I'm going to stay a little longer . . ." I gave a small smile. "Just until you fall asleep." I tiptoed out of the room, closing the bedroom door behind me making sure to leave it a little ajar so that I could easily check in on her.

I checked my phone. There were a few messages from Carmen and a funny video from Pat. *These can wait, nothing too urgent.* I hesitated for a few moments before calling Rick. He picked up right away.

"Hi. It's me. Can you come over to Jackson Heights? It's Mrs. G. She's really ill, Rick. I think I might need your help." I recoiled at the sound of anxiety in my own voice. Without hesitation, Rick responded, "I'll be right over. Text me her address. What do you need me to bring?"

"Just bring yourself."

Rick arrived twenty-five minutes later, armed with two brown paper bags full of food and supplies. He bundled into the cold apartment and placed the bags on the kitchen counter.

"It's freakin' freezing in here. Isn't the heat on?"

I shook my head.

"No wonder she's got pneumonia."

He went in search of a heating thermostat and dialed it up to high. I could see him surveying her surroundings.

"What's she doing in a place like this?"

"You know she went to prison for harbouring illegal aliens in the department store? She came out of prison and went straight into bankruptcy. She lost everything . . . she was just starting to rebuild the business . . . and now this." I stared at the floor, realising for the first time how this might impact my own position.

Rick stepped closer and rubbed my arms up and down.

"Look at you all dressed up in your cute tea party dress." Rick leaned in for a hug. "You're freezing too."

"Never mind me. I'm fine." I pulled away.

Rick got the message. "How is she feeling now?"

"She's sound asleep. But every so often I hear her hacking and . . ." I choked up. "I just don't know what to do Rick--I feel like I should take her to hospital."

Rick stared at me. It certainly was reassuring to have another adult around to help me make some important decisions.

"OK. Let's think about this. She's been to the doc, and he's already prescribed antibiotics for pneumonia? Right?"

"Yes."

"Well, we got to let those pills do the job, y'know?" Rick rubbed my shoulders. "They just need a bit of time to kick in."

"I already know that." I sighed, shrugging off his hands. "Listen to the intensity of that coughing--it's freaking me out a little."

"What do you mean?" Rick appeared concerned.

"But that's not a normal coughing sound!" My voice got higher in pitch. "It sounds more like she had a 40-a-day cigarette habit and I know she's never smoked in her life! She told me so."

Rick's expression took on an altogether more serious look.

"Shh!" I put my finger up to my lips and whispered. "Listen."

My boss had erupted into another violent coughing fit. We both rushed to the door and I opened it wide so that Rick could peek in.

"Who is it?" she called out in a faint voice.

'It's me, Mrs. Gerson. Rick Delgado," he replied. "Willow was worried about you and asked me to come over and check in on you."

Mrs. G. patted the side of the bed and indicated for Rick to sit down. "Come here, young man."

Rick stared at me, seeking my encouragement.

"Go and sit beside her." I urged, shooing him along with my hands.

Looking like a small boy being summoned by the headteacher, he sat on the edge of the bed while I stifled a laugh. He was so out of his big business comfort zone. "I'll make some tea, Mrs. G." I called through, leaving them to it.

It felt intrusive going through her kitchen cupboards once more. I came across a sparse collection of fine china cups, saucers and plates, all of which bore the D'Arcy's emblem--a Hungarian rose, a small tribute to her ancestors. A tear welled up in my eye.

Pull yourself together Willow. She's strong. She's going to be just fine.

I found another tray and laid out the delicate china. Then I found a small packet of chocolate biscuits in one of Rick's paper bags and opened it, placing just one biscuit on the side of the plate. I tread softly over the wooden floorboards in the hallway and stopped for a moment behind the bedroom door, where my soon-to-be ex-husband and boss were in deep conversation.

'It's all my fault, Gigi." Rick was saying. "I messed up."

I put my ear closer to the door and held in a breath.

I couldn't make out what she said back, but I listened as Rick responded. "No. She won't take me back. We're getting a divorce . . ." My spirits sank as I heard Rick say those words out loud.

I cleared my throat, signaling that I was about to enter.

They both stopped talking when I entered the room, leaving me feeling a little on edge.

I sensed Mrs. G's eyes on me as I placed the tray down on her lap and removed the other.

"Thank you, Willow." She threw me a rare smile. I noticed her eyes sunken in her face.

"Rick is keeping me entertained," she said.

He winked at me. He could turn the charisma on and off like a tap. I envied his easy ways.

Mrs. G. shimmied in the bed pulling herself up higher against her pillows. "That's better," she said. "I can breathe easier now. Willow, can you grab me that large manila envelope from the top of the bureau in the living room, please?" Her voice sounded scratchy and the effort of talking tired her.

"Yes," I nodded. "Of course!" Feeling glad to be of use.

I returned a moment later, brandishing the thick envelope.

"Open it and read the first page please."

I stared over at her, then at Rick.

Nervously, I took the paper from the envelope, scanned it then looked at Mrs. G.

"It's a will." I stated, scanning the contents as I spoke.

"This is the reason why I was late this afternoon. I went straight to my lawyer after I saw the doctor."

I was confused.

"But you just have a case of pneumonia--it's not going to kill you." Waves of anxiety began their assault on my stomach.

Mrs. G. coughed again, clearing her throat as she attempted to speak. "I have an underlying health condition." she stated. "I was diagnosed with stage four cancer a few months ago."

Her words hit me like a series of daggers. Before I knew it, Mrs. G. was hugging me tight as my brain absorbed the grim news. I understood exactly what she was telling me, but I refused to take it in. I fell in a heap on her bed, sobbing into her pillow as she hugged me.

"But you can't leave me!" I snorted. "You've been here for me since the day I arrived in D'Arcy's! You've been like a mother to me!" I wailed.

"I had a good life, Willow. Got no regrets." Mrs. G. stroked my hair. "I'm now ready to go."

"But the pop-up stores' What's going to happen to them?" I asked, feeling terrible that I should think of something like that at a time like this.

She wiped the tears off the top of my cheekbones. My green velvet party dress was now speckled with black spots from the mascara that had run. "That's why I called you back. After my funeral, I want you to go to London and launch the UK flagship store."

Our eyes met as I took in the dreadful news. This was her way of saying goodbye to me. We communed in silence. I knew I would never forget that vision of her. Her stare was etched in my memory forever. She was leaving me. I would be in full charge of her empire. I didn't know how I would ever find the courage to be like her--to be as strong as her.

Although the news was shocking, it was clear that Gigi had put a lot of thought into her plans.

I felt Rick gently pulling me back from my boss. He turned me to face him.

"Gigi and I were discussing things while you were making tea." I saw that Rick had been crying too. He stared at her, indicating that he was handing the reigns back to her.

Mrs. G. inhaled deeply, then stared hard at me. "I want you to take over the stores. I want you to build up the pop-up stores, then I want you to purchase D'Arcy's back from the receivers."

Both of them stared at me while I took in the news.

"Buy back D'Arcy's? But how is that even possible?" I said.

Mrs. G didn't say anything but her expression spoke volumes.

"Check the will," Rick urged. "Gigi told me it was all in there."

I read the papers in my hand. I was startled that my name was mentioned on the second line of text.

"There is no reason to think it can't be done." She settled back into her pillows, the last vestiges of energy leaving her as fatigue set in once more. "Isn't that what your little yellow book says?" Her eyes twinkled with mirth.

So, she's been reading my book?

I stared at Rick as he nodded his head in agreement.

"Believe you are and you will be," he said, with one eyebrow raised.

CHAPTER TEN

We Need To Talk About Gigi

True to character, my boss had planned every last detail of her final goodbye. Since her death over a week before, I had tried in vain to find the remaining members of her family, but Mrs. G. had never married or had kids.

Inside the large manila envelope, alongside her will, was a list of instructions. She had wanted an obituary to be posted in the New York Times and had stipulated that flowers should be relinquished in place of charitable donations to a leading cancer charity. She had instructed Tallulah's Tearoom to set aside one of their fine private dining rooms to host a stand-up Hungarian-styled reception.

Apart from a brief stint flying for an airline, her whole life had been dedicated to the running of the family department store in Queens, left to her by her aging parents. There wasn't much in the way of arrangements for me to make, but I couldn't get one thought out of my mind.

How the hell am I going to fulfill her dying wish to earn enough money from the beauty pop-ups to buy D'Arcy's back?

On the morning of the funeral, I rushed around my apartment and scanned my wardrobe for a suitable outfit to wear. Rick had always joked that my 'Widow's Wardrobe' provided enough black attire to dress for a funeral every day of the week.

Audrey Hepburn sang the lyrics to *Moon River* as I settled on a classic 1950s style black dress, complete with black velvet bow at the centre of the waistband. Just like my now ruined green velvet dress, the skirt gently flared out and skimmed just above the knee. I sorted through my canvas bag that held an assortment of opaque black tights and found a pair that hadn't snagged. It was cold outside and I didn't feel like wearing thin nylons. As a representative of Gigi Gerson and her new Plane Jane Beauty Brand, I thought it best to bring the sexy Louboutins out of their box. I practiced walking up and down the narrow hallway but I had yet to master the skill needed to walk in these shoes. At the last minute-- before Rick was due to pick me up, and after calculating that I might be able to wear the Louboutins for a maximum of two hours--I backed down and threw a pair of my trusty Repetto Ballet flats into my bag.

"These will have to do," I sighed.

I wasn't prepared to suffer hours and hours of pain. Looking in the mirror, I decided it was best to keep my makeup as neutral as possible. Waterproof mascara would be an absolute essential on a day like today. I quickly applied a thin cat eye and two coats of Dior show mascara, then put on a sweep of Dolce Vita by Dior lipstick.

I looked at my reflection in the mirror.

I don't know how I am going to get through this.

Faded memories of my parents' funeral suddenly sprung to life. I walked into the kitchen and poured myself a neat brandy. The familiar rolling sensation in my stomach halted temporarily as the heat of the alcohol burned down into my insides. It was a strangely comforting sensation.

'Purely medicinal', I told myself. I smacked my lips, checking the handheld mirror once again for signs of lipstick speckles.

I checked my phone. I saw a heartwarming message from Pat, telling me he was thinking of me and that I had to phone him as soon as it was all over. I smiled. It was so lovely to have him on the other end of the phone. Contact with him had been a lifesaver. Throughout the last few weeks, he had proved to be a great emotional support to me.

Just then the handset lit up. It was Rick. He was waiting for me down-stairs.

This is it, Girl! Showtime!

We drove to St. Patrick's in Brooklyn in silence, neither of us wanting to speak. I caught Rick glancing at me a few times as he navigated the traffic.

"Keep your eyes on the road," I admonished, slinking down further in the leather seat with my fake leopard print fur jacket pulled high, warming my neck while dulling the sound of traffic on the city streets.

"You look like Bet Lynch from Coronation Street with that jacket on."

"How the hell do you know who Bet Lynch is?" I grappled with the idea of Rick watching one of the UK's favourite TV soap operas.

'There's just something about you in that coat-so sexy," he leered. I pushed his hand off the top of my knee.

"Do you ever give up?" I said.

"Nope."

I drew him a look as I pulled my coat tighter around me. "You had your chance." I pretended to brush some invisible crumbs off my dress.

"You know something?" Rick smacked the steering wheel. "This frigid Willow act doesn't work . . . I know you want me."

I don't know if it was the brandy that gave me the courage but I finally gave it to him. "For God's sake! We're going to a funeral! Just shut up and drive!" I demanded.

"OK. OK. Calm down. I was only joking with you." But Rick knew I meant business. He drove on in silence.

I studied the small map of New York City on my phone. "Looks like this is it," I said. St. Paddy's is on the right, where all those black limos are lined up."

The hoi-polloi of New York were gathered at the gates of the church while a group of paparazzi photographers stood off to the side.

I felt relieved. "Looks like Gigi Gerson is going to receive her society send-off after all," I murmured.

The nerves kicked in once more as I became aware that I would have to take the lead in the proceedings.

Rick gripped my hand tight.

"You'll be fine. I'll be by your side . . ." he said.

I turned and hugged him as a pap took our photo but I didn't care.

Inside the cold church, Rick sat at my side on the front pew. I dared not look around. I guessed the fashion crowd would be in attendance and perhaps some of the more notable movers and shakers of the New York scene.

Gigi Gerson had spent her life growing up in the city and, for the most part, was well-liked.

Twenty minutes into the service, I gripped the speech in my sweat-stained hand as Father Joe invited me up to the podium. I was conflicted. It was the moment I had been dreading, but, in the midst of my nerv-ousness, I recognised what an honour it was to stand up there and pay tribute to this remarkable lady who had taken me in, shown me the ropes, and allowed me to flourish under her guidance.

I put one foot in front of the other, careful to walk in my Louboutin's as I tried not to look at who might be staring back at me.

A sea of familiar-looking faces looked on: a few old-timer customers from D'Arcy's, a swathe of ex-employees interspersed with beautiful models accompanied by men who looked like they were old enough to be their fathers.

I began my poem, concentrating on the words in front of me.

"This is 'Foamy Sky' by Hungarian Poet, Miklos Radnoti . . ."

I clutched the paper. Beginning with the words, "The moon sways on a foamy sky, I am amazed that I live." I looked up at the crowd.

Big mistake, Willow. Concentrate on the words.

I regretted downing the brandy. Now I needed to pee.

I got through the evocative words of the poem. Glancing up briefly, I noticed a few mourners in the crowd who appeared to be crying.

Why are they all wearing white gloves? Keep going. Keep concentrating.

I carried on reading the moving words of the poem, relieved to have got through it.

Father Joe nodded in my direction and indicated for me to leave the podium. I stumbled as I made my way back to Rick, daring not to look at anyone but feeling the stares on my face. *Damn shoes.*

My cheeks reddened.

I heard a slow, solitary clapping sound. It took a fleeting second to recognise the striking features of the culprit. It was Jackson. His signature raven-black floppy fringe, hung over one eye.

My heart gave a small leap as he smiled at me. The rest of the church-goers joined in, slowly building in momentum until the whole church exploded into resounding applause. I felt myself shake a little. Sitting down beside Rick, I experienced a strange mix of emotions: excitement and happiness that Jackson had somehow navigated his way back to the USA for his boss's funeral and an aching feeling for the loss of Gigi's life when she still had so much to give. But mostly I was relieved. Relieved that the most nerve-racking part of the day was over. I had done what she asked me to do.

At the graveside, Jackson stood on my left while Rick stood on the right. Both men took my hand in theirs as we watched the grave diggers lower the coffin into the freshly dug soil. I let out a soft sigh--I remembered the day I walked into D'Arcy's Department Store for the first time. I remembered how Jackson told me that I would find a kettle on the fourth floor. I recalled how he found me reading my little yellow book in the store café. How he introduced himself and told me about the vacancy in the beauty hall. My memory flicked back to bumping into Isabella and wanting to make my escape. It all seemed so long ago now.

As the priest said his final words, a slow trickle of tears meandered down my cheek.

Thank God I'm wearing waterproof mascara.

I turned to Jackson. "Do you need to touch up my makeup?"

"You look just fine." He smiled his trademark grin as I gripped his hand tighter.

"Goodbye, Gigi Gerson. I'll never forget you." I said quietly.

And I hope that I can be as brave as you.

Jackson took out a pair of white cotton gloves from inside his jacket and used the cotton finger of one pair to wipe a tear from my face.

"Why does everyone have these gloves on?" I asked, looking up at him. Then it clicked. "Ah! The white glove inspection at D'Arcy's."

"It was Bella's idea." He grimaced, unsure of how I would respond.

"In that case." I said, trying to pull the gloves back off but Jackson stopped me.

"Do it for Gigi." He instructed.

***

Tallulah's Tearoom was abuzz with the glitterati of New York society. All former employees of D'Arcy's Department Store had been invited and everyone had their own version of what it had been like to have been chosen by Mrs. G. as a department store employee. I could tell from many of the famous faces at the wake that quite a few of the ex-employees had gone on to achieve great success in their chosen professions.

But right now, the only person I could focus on was Jackson. He had lit up my day, week . . . no . . . year!

We stood in the centre of the packed dining room, gripping onto each other-eyes shining with delight at being reunited. Rick had wandered off in search of more food and I pounced at the opportunity to be alone with Jackson.

"I saw on Instagram that Gigi had passed away, and it was a no-brainer, I had to fly over." Jackson popped a canapé into his mouth with signature aplomb.

"But where have you been all this time?" I asked.

"Dublin, darling. Trying to make a name for myself," he cackled as he threw back a swig of champagne.

"That makes so much sense!" I put two and two together. "The last point of entry! The immigration officer told me that--said you would be returned to the last place you left!" I shook my head in disgust. "I'm so stupid--I could have found you earlier."

Don't worry, babes." He put his arm around my shoulder and hugged me in tight. "I had a lot of stuff to sort out when I got home. Basically, I had to start from scratch." Jackson looked humbled. I felt bad. Real bad. It was all my fault that he got deported.

How can I ever repay him?

Lightning struck.

"The London store! I'm going to need a manager for the London store!" I murmured.

"What?" Jackson looked down at me. "What are you blabbering about?"

I looked up at him. "Before she died, Gigi tasked me with opening up a series of pop-up stores in a few of the major cities around the world. I've just launched San Francisco, and next on my list is London and New York."

Jackson's eyes twinkled.

"You mean she trusted *you* to do all *that?*" he smirked.

"No, seriously . . . you want me to be your London manager?"

"Yes!" There was not a trace of doubt in my mind whatsoever. "I do!"

He scratched his chin, "Well, I'll just have to have a wee think about that, won't I?" Jackson turned his back on me, took a few steps away, stared at me, then returned.

Ever the bloody showman!

"It's a deal." He shook my hand in agreement. "Oh, but I have just one caveat."

"What's that?"

Uh-oh! Here we go! The diva is back!

"You must let me pick my own team."

My heart sank a little. "I don't know about that Jackson," I said, sadly. "Mrs. G. specifically requested that *I* had to recruit all the staff."

"Oh. I get that, darling . . ." His facial expression serious. "You can still fly over and go through the motions but I'll make the final decision on who I work with."

I hesitated. I wanted to help Jackson but at the same time, I didn't want to go against my boss's dying wishes.

He sensed my hesitation and put a hand on his hip. "Look. I recommended you, didn't I?"

I nodded my head.

Jackson surveyed the scene at Tallulah's. "And that turned out spectacularly well, didn't it?"

I nodded again and smirked.

"So, let me do this. Do you need time to consult your little yellow book?" he asked.

I burst out laughing, spurting out the remnants of the champagne in my mouth.

"Can't take you bloody anywhere!" Jackson dabbed the spilt champagne off my coat, searching my eyes with his.

"How do you get through the day, Willow?"

I swiped his arm playfully causing him to drop his champagne flute. The glass shattered in tiny shards all over the tiled floor as a hush swept over the room, causing everyone to stare at us.

I swept in and took my moment.

"Ladies and gentlemen, allow me to introduce you to Jackson Dart, the newly appointed manager of Gigi's London store," I declared.

The wake gatherers began to holler and clap their approval. I could recognise Rick in the back cheering as well.

Many of them knew Jackson from having worked beside him in

D'Arcy's. He was a hard guy to miss.

Jackson blushed then took a bow. He was quite clearly in his element.

Just then a vivacious-looking redhead made her entrance in Tallulah's. It was Carlotta Rossellini. The world-famous makeup artist who had been the judge at The New York Makeup Artistry Competition.

I drew in a deep breath as she stepped towards me.

"My darling! I'M EVER SO SORRY I MISSED GIGI'S FUNERAL!" she screeched, breathing alcohol fumes all over me. "My flight was late. So sorry!" She air-kissed me before navigating her way through the crowd in the direction of a group of exquisite-looking models standing at the marble gin bar.

"Bollocks!" Jackson bent down to whisper in my ear. "Don't believe a word she says. She was sitting up in First on my flight yesterday. She tried to pretend she didn't know me."

I hoped Carlotta hadn't heard him but I wondered why she would miss the funeral of such a close friend.

"Never mind that." I gave my head a tiny shake. "She's here now I suppose." Part of me was disappointed in Carlotta.

Maybe she was a fair-weather friend?

I felt bad for Gigi.

A group of waiters and waitresses made their entrance, all dressed in traditional black and white and carrying silver platters of sour soup that had been a custom of Hungarian funerals. By the look on some mourners' faces, it looked like this was the last thing they wanted to taste but Mrs. G. had insisted that the soup be served.

Rick appeared at my side, holding his bowl and displaying a look of disgust on his face.

"Don't say anything. Just eat up." I commanded. I also attempted to try it but it wasn't to my liking. As we were deciding what to do with the offending soup, I felt a tap on my shoulder.

"Willow!"

I was shocked to see Jake standing in front of me.

Oh, for fuck's sake.

"Jake!" I grabbed his arm.

"Glad to see you could make it to *this* funeral." he sniffed.

I'm so not in the mood to deal with you . . .I never met your brother or any of your family... now's the time to change into the Repettos.

"Jackson, c'mere!" I grabbed his jacket. "Meet Jake." I indicated for him to take over from me. "I have to go now, sorry!" I dashed off, moving through the crowd.

I rushed to the 'Ladies,' barged in and found an empty cubicle to hide in. I placed the lid down, wiped it with a sanitising wipe and sat down. It was good to take the weight off my feet for a few moments. I dug into my bag and changed out of my shoes for the ballet flats. My phone pinged. It was Jackson telling me to hurry up and rejoin the party. I texted back telling him to give me a few more minutes.

I dragged myself out of the cubicle, returned to the vanity and reapplied my lipstick, then spritzed Terre by Hermes all over me. It didn't matter that it was a fragrance for men--the notes of citrus and wood enlivened me.

I took a deep breath and examined my reflection in the mirror. Mixing brandy with champagne had not been one of my best ideas. My head was starting to swirl as another message from Jackson arrived.

"Hurry up and get out here. Hot guy has just arrived. I need my wing woman."

I smiled and texted back. "Be right there."

Nothing else for it but to get back out there and face the music. I smoothed my hair and swung my coat over my shoulders. I had lost a few inches in height by changing my shoes but the alcohol was helping me to feel invincible. I had no clue what I would say to Jake but at least I wouldn't be alone. I could bank on Jackson helping me out, if necessary.

I stepped out of the sanctuary of the 'Ladies' room and straight into

Jackson's arms.

"I made my escape." Jackson rolled his eyes. "How long did you go out with him for?"

"Don't ask. I was on the rebound."

"That's what they all say, ye of little taste." He grabbed my hand and pulled me in the direction of the Gin Bar. "You need a top-up."

It felt so good to be in the company of my best friend, especially on such a sad day.

"God, I missed you!" Jackson swooped down and hugged me tight, squeezing the breath out of me. He kissed me on the cheek then turned to order another round of drinks.

It had been a long day and the copious amounts of alcohol I had consumed was starting to make me feel sleepy.

I tapped Jackson on the shoulder while he waited to be served at the bar.

"Where are you staying tonight?"

"Well, I was thinking of your couch," Jackson said, hopeful. "That is, if you'll have me."

"Yes. Of course. I've always got space for you--it's the least I can do." I said.

"Where do you live now?" He turned towards me with an overflowing tray full of drinks.

"Oh, you know," I tried to play it cool, "Madonna's old building in Hell's Kitchen."

"Well, well, well," he gasped. "You don't say! I always knew you would do well."

"Jake found it for me."

"Why am I not surprised," he tutted.

I was confused. "What do you mean?"

"Everyone at D'Arcy's knew he had the hots for you. You were the only one who didn't notice," he said.

"I did try to make it work..." I said, "but . . ." I looked away.

"Let me guess." He laughed a little, easing my discomfort. "Way too old-fashioned for my Willow?" He picked up his bag and said his good-byes before pushing me towards the exit.

Carlotta grabbed me by the arm. "Wait, you guys! Don't go yet." She paused. "We need to have a talk, darling." She held my gaze as we spoke. In the sharp light of day, I could tell she was older than I first thought. Her lined face was filled with layers of foundation and the cigarette lines had taken up residence all around her pouty, painted lips.

She took a sip from her champagne glass then said in a low voice, "We need to talk about Gigi."

I agreed. "Yes, we do." I took out my business card from my bag and handed it to her. "I agree, but first I have to talk to someone else. Excuse me!"

I laced my arm in Jackson's and pulled him over in the direction of the piano where Rick was holding court with a blonde-haired waitress. I took out my phone and tapped him on the shoulder.

"Hi." I put my phone under his nose and smiled at the waitress. "We just got our court date in." I smiled. The waitress drew daggers at Rick. I wondered what yarn he had been spinning for her.

"He's all yours," I said, as Jackson and I strode away through the crowd.

"Now show me this 'hot' guy," I demanded.

We laughed and giggled as arm-in-arm we tore through the tearooms trying to find the 'Brad Pit' lookalike that Jackson had his eye on . . . to no avail.

There was no sign of him anywhere. We spotted Isabella de la Souza off in the distance but mutually agreed to body-swerve her.

I turned and stared at Jackson. "I guess we should just go home."

Jackson stared down at me. "You sure?"

I nodded. It had been a long day and now I just wanted to sleep.

"Yes," he said.

Jackson let out a huge sigh and shook his head. "Thank God you said that . . . I'm running on jet lag and alcohol fumes at the moment." He bent his head down towards me and hugged me tight.

"God. I missed you, Willow."

After a long, comforting hug we pulled apart. I looked up and saw Patrick staring straight at us--a look of fury on his face.

"Great. Just great. I flew all the way over here to support you but it looks like you don't need anything from me." He turned and stormed off, tearing through the crowd to get away from me.

"Wait! . . . that's the guy I was talking about," Jackson pointed after him.

"Hold this!" I slammed my coat and bag into Jackson's arms and rushed towards the exit of the tearooms. My heart was racing in my chest as I rushed out of the building into the cold dark street beyond. There was no sign of Patrick. He had bolted leaving me with no opportunity to explain.

It was freezing out on the sidewalk as I stamped my feet in frustration. I texted him five times, but he didn't respond.

Bloody hell . . . why won't you answer me?

There was nothing else for it but to go back into the tearooms and fetch Jackson.

CHAPTER ELEVEN

Meet Me At The Langham

My phone pinged. It was Patrick. In the dim light of the bathroom, I read his message.

"Meet me at The Langham."

I exhaled then began to giggle. The thought of seeing him again filled me with anticipation. We would make up and get back on track, of that I was sure.

I glanced at the mirror one more time, fixed my lipstick and smoothed my hair, then left the apartment.

I sent a quick text to Jackson to let him know I would catch up with him later. I guessed he was just fine sleeping on the couch.

Back out in the city streets, I made my way down Fifth. I guessed it would take me ten minutes to arrive at the hotel on foot. I figured no point in trying to hail a cab.

I strode straight up to the reception desk and waited in line, all the while scanning the lobby for signs of Patrick. I watched on as a host of Wine Industry expo attendees flocked in and out of the hotel, all carrying the same white bags.

Finally, it was my turn.

"Good evening, madam. How can I help you?" asked the receptionist.

"I'm here to meet Patrick Brodie, do you mind letting him know that I've arrived?"

The receptionist checked the computer screen, placing her hand in front of her mouth as she searched for his name.

How many Patrick Brodie's can there be? Surely he would use his real name and not a pseudonym?

"Aha! Found him!" She smiled back at me.

She picked up the phone and then looked up at me.

"And your name is?"

"Willow Campbell." I smiled.

"Mr. Brodie, I have a Willow Campbell to see you in reception, Sir."

There was a pause as she looked up at me as she listened to him speak. My stomach lurched.

"Shall I send Ms. Campbell up, Sir?"

She placed the handset down.

"Room 777." She instructed.

"Thank you! Thank you so much!" I beamed, my heart racing as I darted towards the elevator door.

For once, I was glad that the elevator interior was smoked glass. I didn't have to look at my reflection under the harsh glare. My phone pinged, it was Jackson wishing me good luck.

Out on the seventh floor, I slowed my pace as I neared his room door. My heart was racing.

Can't believe he's flown in to support me.

Then I quietly knocked on the door. Patrick pulled the door open. I lunged at him, throwing my arms around his neck, my emotions spinning out of control at the thought of being with him again. I held his cheeks in the palm of my hands and kissed him hard, taking him by surprise.

"Daddy! Is this the lady you were telling me about?"

Patrick prised himself apart from me as he stared down at a little blonde girl.

"Yes, darling. This is Willow." I took a moment to get myself together.

"I thought you told me you were just friends." Coco looked confused, as she eyed me up and down.

Godammit. Nice one, Patrick. You brought your daughter.

I bent down to his daughter's height and held out my hand to shake hers.

"And you must be Coco." I said.

Her sticky hand pawed mine. "Coco Belle Brodie."

"Nice to meet you, Coco."

Patrick shifted uneasily from one foot to the other. He held out his arms in an apology, shaking his head.

"You know the score . . . couldn't get a babysitter and my parents are in town for the wine conference."

"Oh! I see." All my plans in the romance department were completely dashed.

"How long are you here for?" I asked.

"Just for the weekend." He looked down at his daughter who was sidled up beside him, tugging onto his trouser leg. "I can't keep Coco out of school, so we're flying back on Sunday afternoon.

I knew I should be glad that he was here, that I at least got to spend some time with him, but I hadn't anticipated that he would bring his little daughter with him.

I sat down on the armchair, not quite sure how to navigate being around a small child.

"So, Coco, how do you like being in New York?" I said.

What a stupid question to ask a six-year-old.

I heard the flush of the toilet in the adjoining bathroom. I looked at Patrick with eyebrows raised.

An apologetic expression stretched across his face as a woman in her early 60s made an appearance in the room.

"Mom, this is Willow."

***

Three hours later, Pat dropped me off at my apartment in a cab.

As I stepped out of the taxi, he peered up at me from its dark interior. He shouted through the window.

"Nine am sharp, don't be late." He winked.

I stepped into my building, took the elevator, didn't bother to check my appearance in the mirror, then stumbled into my apartment and threw myself down on the couch.

"Well, well, well . . . look at what the cat dragged in."

Jackson stood in the doorway of my bedroom, drawing me a smirk as he spoke. "Thanks a bloody million for leaving me." He pretended to be annoyed with me.

"I take it you found your man?" he said.

"I did indeed." I laughed, giddy with delight.

"And . . . ?" said Jackson.

"And what?" I replied.

"Don't give me that coy look. Doesn't work with me. Did you do the dirty deed?"

I picked up a cushion and threw it at him, he dodged it and threw it back at me, whacking me in the face. I held the cushion up at my face and spoke in a low voice. "His mum and daughter were in the room."

Jackson leaned down and pulled the cushion away from me. "Did I hear you right? He's got a daughter?"

Jackson threw himself down on the couch beside me. "What the fuck? I mean how are you going to navigate that?"

I shook my head, sobering up in an instant. "I don't know."

"Taking on someone else's kid is kinda a big deal."

I turned and stared at him. "Don't you think I've been thinking that?"

Jackson put his arm around me and hugged me.

"I think I've finally met the *one* . . . but it's a lot to consider," I said.

"Hold your horses. It wasn't so long ago that you thought Rick was the 'one' and look how that turned out . . . then you went straight into a relationship with Jake, who no doubt wanted you barefoot and pregnant...."

I burst out laughing. I could always depend on Jackson to see things as clear as day.

"OK, 'nuff about me, what about you? Did you meet anyone in Dublin?"

I wanted to change the subject and keep all the details about Patrick and I to myself, but how I missed our midnight chats, sitting on the couch, cups of tea warming our hands as we set the world to rights into the wee hours. I went into the kitchen to boil the kettle.

Jackson called through, "You still reading the 'yellow book?'"

"Nope. I gave up all that nonsense a long time ago."

I handed a mug of tea to Jackson and stuck out my bottom lip. Jackson sat up, tucking his knees under his chin, his black hair falling over one eye. His black eyeliner now smudged.

"So. What are you going to do?" He took a sip of the hot tea.

"About Patrick?" I looked off into the distance. "I don't know. I don't know if I see myself as 'mother material'"

"Oh, Willow . . ." Jackson sighed, "why do you doubt yourself so much?"

"I don't know." I fiddled with the mug, deep in thought.

Jackson placed his mug down and moved in closer to me. "OK. Let me ask you this . . . would you have had a child with Rick . . . if things had turned out better?"

"When I was in the relationship, I was in it 100%." I declared.

But Jackson wasn't finished. "That's not the answer. I'm asking if you would have had a baby with Rick? Tell me the truth, Willow, this is important . . . I'm trying to help you here."

I looked up at him and shook my head. "No."

Jackson let a loud sigh. "Good. Now we're getting somewhere."

He stood up and strode around the room, arms folded, deep in thought.

I began to giggle to myself.

God! How I've missed these nights.

He stopped what he was doing and scolded me. "This ain't funny lady. I'm trying to sort your life out . . . make sure you don't make the same mistakes over and over."

"OK. You have my full attention. But first can you give me five minutes to change into my pj's?" I said.

"Go ahead." Jackson nodded, placing the cups of tea in the kitchen sink before fetching two wine glasses from the cupboard. "Hurry up, now!"

Ten minutes later, I re-entered the living room, wrapped in a thick pink fleece dressing gown to the sound of Burt Bacharach singing *This Guy's in love with you*.

It was one of those perfect moments: the mood, the music, the company.

I beamed my approval at Jackson. He knew me so well.

I had to hand it to him. He was a natural with people. He could parlay himself into any given situation. He was one of those rare people who had a natural gift for making others feel instantly at home.

I bent down and kissed him on the cheek.

"It's been quite the day, hasn't it?" I sighed as my mind flicked over the funeral and my messy reunion with Pat.

"I'm going to miss Mrs. G." I said.

Jackson looked away. "We're all going to miss her."

"But I'm going to miss you even more." I looked down at him as he sat on my couch. I was happy in the knowledge that now he was back in my life, I was never going to lose touch with him ever again.

"When you were out, Carlotta Rossellini phoned you on the landline." Jackson shifted uneasily, eyeing me from under his black fringe.

"She did? What did she say?"

"She was looking to hire some makeup artists for . . . er, London Fashion Week in February." Jackson found it difficult to suppress his excitement.

"Shut up! No way!" My stomach lurched. It had always been one of my long-held dreams to work the London shows.

"And? So, what happened?"

Jackson beamed. "She just booked me to work at the February shows in London."

"What? You're working London Fashion Week?"

He nodded.

I threw everything down on the counter and ran to him. "That's wonderful!" I shouted, hugging him, even though I felt a stab of jealousy in my stomach.

Jackson looked down at me. "Are you sure you're OK with it? I know it's been your dream for like . . ." Jackson threw up his arms, "ever!"

"I'm over the blinkin' moon for you, silly." I tapped him on the arm, in a vain attempt to cover up my envy.

"Are you sure? You're not pissed off or annoyed and just putting on that famous "Willow brave face?" He crossed his arms, searching my face for any signs of anger or jealousy.

"Look." I pointed to the Edie Sedgewick calendar on the kitchen wall. I stared at the blocked-out dates where I had scrawled the words "London Pop-Up Store Opening," which coincided with the dates for the fashion show.

We stared at each other as the dates sank in.

"We're going to be in London at the same time!" I laughed. Jackson hugged me and we both squealed. We just couldn't contain our excitement. "Do you think Mrs. G. engineered this from above?"

"Who knows?" Jackson held my hands in his, smiling at me, "But knowing Mrs. G. and her wily ways . . . it wouldn't surprise me in the slightest."

I really didn't want to ask the next question but the words blurted out of my mouth before I could stop myself.

"Did Carlotta . . . er . . . did she ask about me?" I twirled my hair as I spoke, mad at myself for asking the question in the first place.

Jackson's expression changed. "She didn't. No . . . sorry."

My spirits sank.

"She probably thought you would be too busy with running the business for Gigi." Jackson tried his best to placate. He put his arm around me.

"Don't worry, babes. Your time will come . . . one day." He pinched my cheek, "You've got rather a lot going on right now."

"Yeah. You're right." I gathered up our glasses. It had been a long day and now I just wanted to go to sleep. I stood in the shadow of the doorway. "So, you're really leaving tomorrow?" I was just getting used to being back in his company.

"I have to, babes. They only allowed me in, so I could attend the funeral. I'm flying back with Carlotta." He stared at me, checking my response. "We're going to be flying back in First. She booked me on her business expense account."

"You sneaky git!" I threw a pillow at him. "Sleeping with the enemy!"

"Hardly." He took a gulp of the hot tea, smacked his lips then drew me a wicked glare. "Think of it more like I'm your spy. She trusts me."

I switched the living room light off.

"Good night, Jackson. Love you."

He blew me a kiss. "Love you too." I padded off to my bedroom, happy in the knowledge that I had my old friend back. I stopped in my tracks as I heard the lyrics to *Harvest Moon* by Neil Young emanating softly from the living room. I smiled to myself. It was Jackson's favourite song.

***

The next morning, I awoke at 7:15. My tongue felt like sandpaper as I searched my bed for my phone. There was a stream of text messages from Patrick, *thanking* me for the evening before.

I threw on my dressing gown and knocked on the living room door.

"Are you decent?" I called through, scrambling to throw some layers on. The temperature had plummeted to 10 below and it didn't feel much warmer than that inside my apartment.

"Come in," he said.

"I'm just going to pop out and get us some breakfast, do you want anything?" I grabbed my purse from the coffee table.

"A lox bagel? I haven't had one of those since . . . well, you know." Jackson shrugged.

"No problem." I smiled at him. His hair was messed up and he wore a tired expression. "How did you sleep last night?"

"Like a baby," he said.

I noticed a small tub of pills on the floor at his feet.

"What are those?" I asked.

"Those?" his eyes followed mine, "ach . . . they're just something I got off the doctor to help me sleep," he explained.

I sat down on the armchair. "Is everything alright, Jackson?"

"What do you mean?" he grew antsy, shifting on the couch.

"I don't know . . . you appear to have lost a lot of weight." I checked him up and down as he sat on the couch, There wasn't an ounce of fat on him.

"You jealous or something?" Jackson looked me up and down, "you're putting the beef on again, Willow."

His words stung as he expertly shifted the focus off himself onto me.

"Sorry. Shouldn't have said that," he said.

"It's OK. I know my own body. I don't need to be told by anyone when I've put on weight." I scolded, and I got up and left the room.

I made my way straight to the bathroom and pulled out the dreaded scales. I stood on them and watched on in horror. Even when I subtracted two pounds for the clothes I was wearing, the number was offensive to me.

"My God!" I gasped. "He's right!"

I turned to face Jackson, he held out his hand to me. "Want one?

They'll help you kick it off again."

I pushed his hand away and stormed off, "No. I bloody well do not. I'll do it the hard way. Just like everything else in my bloody life."

Jackson called after me. "Willow! Don't be like that."

A half-hour later, I returned to find Jackson deep in conversation on his cell. I placed the bagel on a plate and popped the coffee on a tray, handing it to Jackson as he ended his call. "Eat that." I scowled. "You need it." My mind was whirring overtime. This was bad.

"That was Carlotta. I'm staying at her Richmond mews house in London for the duration of the shows," he said.

"That's so great!" I hugged Jackson. "Everything's looking up for you now." His good news was tainted by the earlier pill-popping discovery.

Jackson leaned in and hugged me. "Are you sure you're OK with it? I mean I know how much you've wanted this." He looked concerned.

"It's fine. Really. You deserve it." I placed my shopping bag down on the kitchen counter. "Just be sure you don't forget me when you're a famous makeup artist flying all over the world."

"I won't." He drew me a rueful smile.

"And promise you'll meet me in London when I fly over to launch the store?" I stood with my hands on my hips. "You promised you'd be my manager, remember?"

"I do recall," he laughed.

I could tell his mind was elsewhere. A nagging thought tugged at me.

Once he gets a taste of working the shows is he going to settle down to working in the pop-up store every day?

Jackson began to pack his bag as I cleared up the breakfast dishes. The familiar sinking feeling, that I tried so hard to keep at bay, engulfed my spirits.

I checked the time. Patrick would be arriving in the next half hour and I looked like a sack of potatoes.

Time to put on the pan stick & spackle.

CHAPTER TWELVE

Number One Girl

I stood on the sidewalk, wrapped in my down-filled puffer coat, and pulled my woollen hat over my ears. My fingers were as cold as ice inside my mittens and the wind chill made the temperature feel like it was-15 degrees.

East coast winters could be brutal at the best of times but today felt particularly cold.

A taxi pulled up and Patrick stepped out to allow me to climb in.

He indicated at Coco who was sitting in the back seat of the car.

"I hope you don't mind? My mom had to attend a meeting in the city . . . we . . . um . . . dropped her off en route." Patrick wore an apologetic expression while I attempted to conceal my surprise.

This wasn't what we planned.

I stared at him. "Wish you had given me some advance notice," I said.

He shrugged his shoulders as I attempted to climb in but Coco blocked my way.

"Move up, darling and let Willow sit beside you." Patrick called through the window to her. I could hear the exasperation in his voice as he attempted to save face in front of me.

Coco sulked, crossed her arms across her red anorak and refused to budge. I stood and stared at Patrick as he stared back. "Sorry. She's not usually this obstinate."

A brittle laugh escaped me as I stared back. "I guess she's not used to sharing you with anyone." The sentence was a cross between a question and a statement.

"I guess not."

The taxi driver called back to Coco. "Move up little lady and let your mom and pop sit beside you."

"She's not my mom!" shouted Coco.

I felt like my heart missed a beat as Coco began to cry.

Shit! Should I just leave now?

I gripped onto Patrick's elbow and stared hard at him. "I'm not so sure this is such a good idea." I tried to put myself into Coco's little shoes as my mind raced back to past events in my own life. Passed about from pillar to post after the death of my own parents. I had a deep knowledge of how it felt to have lost parents at such a young age . . . I knew this situation was going to be way more difficult than her dad anticipated.

"Maybe we should just call the whole thing off." I blurted, at once annoyed with myself for saying what I thought out loud.

Patrick was having none of it. "No, no way. We're not giving in to a six-year-old," he declared. He turned to his daughter and spoke to her in a stern but steady voice. "Coco. If you do not move along the seat this instant, then you're not going to the zoo."

Coco bit her lip then let out a huge sigh. "OK, Daddy."

Patrick turned and smiled at me, "Negotiations always work." He laughed, but I didn't laugh with him.

Maybe I should have spent the morning with Jackson after all.

The journey from Hell's Kitchen to Bronx Zoo took just under 40 minutes. Patrick and I chatted while Coco rode in silence. I wondered how it was possible for a little girl to stay in a mood for so long then I remembered my own childhood. I was a class act at pulling that stunt.

I began to giggle.

"What's so funny?" Patrick asked.

I shook my head. "Nothing really." I drew Coco a sideways look then giggled some more.

You've met your match, Coco-Belle Brodie.

At the zoo, the baby doll sheep proved to be the highlight of Coco's day as she stood in front of them, talking to them in her little girl's voice. I watched on, arm-in-arm with Patrick, as she took photos of the sheep with her little Instamatic camera.

"That little lady's going to be a famous photographer when she grows up." He beamed with pride as he watched over her. "Takes it from her mother."

I looked up at Patrick and pulled him in tighter. "Tell me about Natalie."

Deep in thought, he was silent for a second or two. "She was a beauty. Long dark hair. Italian blood, I think." I looked on at Coco's luscious blonde locks, then at Patrick. He knew what I was thinking. "Yeah, she took her colouring from me."

"She's a little beauty." I offered.

"Just like her mom." He took out a small passport sized photo of his wife and showed it to me. "This is Nat."

I stared at her. I thought my heart was flipping inside my chest. She was a natural beauty. In the photo she didn't wear a scrap of makeup but her vitality shone through.

"I'm sorry you lost her." I stared up at him. He put the photo away and avoided my gaze.

"Me too."

We walked on arm-in-arm as we followed Coco scamper around the animal pens. My mind raced at the thought of taking Patrick and his daughter on.

Was I capable of it? Did I even want to?

We had only just met and yet here I was speculating over a future together.

Is he doing the same thing?

Coco refused to warm to me, no matter how hard I tried to win her over.

I sensed that Patrick regretted his decision to bring us together so soon. We walked arm-in-arm as Coco ran ahead of us.

"The last six years can't have been easy." I looked up into Pat's eyes and caught a look of pain as he winced at the memory.

"No. It hasn't." I heard him sigh.

"I mean, she's so used to just having you around and I guess she doesn't want to share you with anyone." I knew I was playing devil's advocate. I also knew I was testing him to see how he would respond.

Patrick grabbed me and pulled me in close, "She's just going to have to get used to us." His eyes searched mine. "Right?"

I nodded as Patrick stole a kiss. I opened my eyes fleetingly to see Coco stare at us. I could tell the fight was clearly on.

***

By 12:30 we were done with the zoo. No number of cute animals could stop Coco's whining about wanting her grandma and wanting to go back to the hotel. She sat opposite us in the zoo café, clutching her hot chocolate between her tiny palms, her pink nail varnish was chipped in places and her long blonde hair looked like it could do with a good brushing. She had the same green eyes as her father and wrinkled her nose in an identical fashion. The scattering of freckles across her nose and cheekbones hinted at carefree days in the Californian sunshine.

"So, what do you think of New York, Coco? Do you like it." I asked, glancing at Patrick as he drank the last residues of coffee.

"Not really." She twiddled a five-dollar note in her fingers. "Daddy, can I spend this now? Can we go to the store? Pleeese! I wanna buy sheeps."

"You mean you want to buy a sheep." Her dad corrected her.

Patrick knocked his knee against mine then drew me a look.

I took out my phone and showed her some photos. "Look, this is where I come from."

She glanced at the photos in a disinterested manner then began to brighten. "You have baby doll sheeps in Scotland?" her eyes shone with excitement.

"Yes, we do," I declared, thankful that I had taken photos of livestock on a local farm visit many moons ago.

Patrick elbowed me. "Well done, Willow," he whispered, glad that I had finally made a connection with his daughter.

But just as quickly as she had shown some kind of interest, Coco reverted to sulking.

"Can we go home now Daddy, please," she wailed. "I'm cold."

I stood up. "Yes. Let's." I grabbed my Kate Spade and zipped up the jacket.

I was as relieved as Coco to get the day trip over with.

"Nice bottle of Chardonnay chilling in the fridge right about now," I said, but he didn't hear me. He was walking Coco in the direction of the zoo store. I followed on as my mind wandered back to Jackson. I envisaged him being at the airport and getting ready to check-in for his flight to London. The discovery of those pills had left me with an unsettled feeling.

I stared over at Patrick and his daughter as they perused the stuffed toy sheep in the store. From where I was standing, this little slice of family life looked like it could be hard work. And there was Jackson flying back to the UK to work the shows with the renowned Makeup artist, Carlotta Rossellini at the helm.

"Shall we?" Patrick beamed at me as he headed back in my direction holding Coco's hand. She held the stuffed sheep in her free hand, swinging it back and forward, pleased with herself in that she had managed to get what she wanted. The three of us walked into the frigid cold air.

"Penny for them?" Patrick said.

I shook my head and forced a smile, "It's nothing really . . . I was . . . er . . . daydreaming." I knew he would be leaving soon. Going back to his hectic family life in San Francisco, while I was faced with going back to my Hell's Kitchen apartment . . . alone.

Out of nowhere, a tear meandered down my frozen cheek.

I heard Coco ask her daddy why the 'lady' was crying.

Patrick wrapped his arms tightly around me, "What's wrong? Did I say something to upset you?"

I felt stupid.

"It's fine." I shook my head. "It's probably just the events of yesterday catching up on me."

Patrick believed me as he hugged me tighter.

"Grief comes on like that." He placed his fingers under my chin and raised my head. "You just never know when it's going to hit you," he said.

"I know. I wasn't much older than Coco when I lost my own parents," I said, staring at Patrick.

"I see." Patrick looked uncomfortable. "Look. I guess this has all been too much too soon. I'm sorry for putting all of us on you."

Is he having second thoughts?

"I'm going to take Coco back to the hotel. Apart from *'the sheeps'* I guess she hasn't had such a great time of it."

Patrick appeared flustered as he navigated his way towards the exit with his daughter, while I trailed on behind them.

The energy between us was strange and the butterflies in my stomach sprang into life.

Is he dumping me?

I walked behind them, my thoughts racing, and then Patrick stopped in his tracks to take a call. I waited and watched while Coco laced her arms through his legs, circling and stopping every few moments to stick her tongue out at me. I tried not to pay much attention to Coco or the conversation. I was too cold and uncomfortable to care.

Patrick turned to look at me, his complexion was ashen. "That was my mom. She's in a taxi. She'll be here any minute. Kate's had a heart attack and she's in the ICU. We're flying back tonight."

I held my hand over my mouth. "Oh my God, Patrick. I'm so sorry."

Although she was employed as the housekeeper, I knew that Kate held a pivotal position in the family dynamics. She did everything for them: from cooking to cleaning to babysitting Coco.

"Tell me, what can I do to help?" I stared up at him, daring not to believe that we could be over before we even had a chance to begin.

"I don't know Willow. It's just such a shock . . . she's been like a mother to me."

"Daddy? Who are you talking about?" Coco picked up on our concern. "Daddy, what is it?"

He knelt down to her height. "Everything's OK," he told her.

"But Daddy, why are you crying?" She wiped a tear away with her finger.

"I'm not crying, Coco." He pretended to joke. "The cold air is making me cry, you know how sometimes that happens?" He rubbed his hand up and down her arm. "C'mon let's get you back to the hotel, we need to pack."

I watched on, detached from the gentle father-daughter scene in front of me.

Think Willow. Do something. He's leaving.

But I didn't do anything. I stood on the sidewalk and watched as a taxi screeched to a halt outside the zoo. I saw Vivian wave over. Patrick placed Coco in the back seat with her grandma then rushed over to hug me.

"I'll call you as soon as we land."

In his rush to get away, Patrick had forgotten to kiss me. He sent me a text five minutes later, apologizing. I told him it didn't matter.

I hated myself for being so bloody understanding all the time.

The fact that he rushed off without so much as a 'goodbye kiss' did matter. It mattered a lot.

***

The days that followed were filled with lots of soul-searching, doubt and anxiety as I collaborated with George on the recruitment campaigns for both the New York and London stores.

Patrick and I exchanged texts every evening mostly before the start of his evening shift at the bar, when he would keep me updated on Kate's recovery. She was going to make it but had a long road to recovery ahead of her. He had no idea when he would be able to fly back over to New York and my work schedule was jam-packed for the foreseeable future.

At night, alone in my apartment, my mind often flicked back to our time on the beach. I still had the soft white pebbles that I had snuck into my pocket--a souvenir of our short time together.

Why are my romances so fleeting? Why am I not capable of meeting someone who's in it for the long haul?

The days were easier than the nights. They were filled with activity. In fact, to an outsider looking in, I was the picture of the perfect career woman about town, gadding about here, there, and everywhere, fetching coffees, discussing plans with interior designers, and talking over budgets with accountants and architects.

Patrick sounded like he was as busy as me. Not only did he have his usual workdays in San Francisco, managing Brodie's Bar, but he was also trying to take care of the day-to-day upkeep of the house and winery. It was a massive workload for anyone, never mind a single dad with a six-year-old daughter to take care of.

In stark contrast, Jackson's text messages sounded like he was on a different planet altogether. He was constantly out socializing with

180

Carlotta's team of makeup artists and hobnobbing with celebrities while attending fashion shoots.

I gulped back a glass of red wine and re-read Jackson's text message.

'Heading over to the Ivy to have lunch with Daphne, then we're going for drinks at the Smokehouse."

So bloody jealous!

From what I could gather, Daphne was the Creative Director of an up-and-coming fashion house and Jackson appeared to be smitten with her. She appeared to have a lot of power and influence and, knowing Jackson so well, I knew he would be under her spell.

So far, she had booked him on two fashion shoots for some high-end British magazines, and she had promised to keep him busy for the next few months. There was talk of the Paris shows too.

". . . she says If I do well at the London shows there's a chance I can go over to Paris."

I took another gulp. The reality of his ascending career projection hit me hard.

He's never going to come and work for me in the London store now.

I guessed it was time to start looking for an Assistant Manager.

Best be on the safe side.

These two worlds were poles apart and I appeared to be stuck in the middle, all the while trying to decide which direction I wanted to go in.

As the shows beckoned, I made arrangements to fly to London. I didn't tell Patrick I was going, I thought it best to just let our little romance peter out.

'No hard feelings if it doesn't work out.'

If I recall correctly, that's what I said to him that night at San Francisco International Airport.

***

Carmen checked in regularly with progress reports on the San Francisco boutique. I bit my tongue each time she emailed, stopping me from asking how Patrick was doing.

It's not professional, Willow. Don't bring her into it.

I picked up the phone and called Carmen.

Five minutes into our call, she asked me the question I had been dreading.

"So? How's the romance going?" she said.

I was glad we weren't on a video call as my expression would have given the game away.

"Oh, you know, we're taking things real slow . . ." I tapped my pen on my notepad.

"Mmm ," she mumbled.

I could tell Carmen wasn't buying it. She was a shrewd one.

"There's something I've been meaning to tell you . . . I don't know how to say this . . . but I feel that I should."

"Go on . . ." My heart started to beat faster as I braced myself.

"Since Pat arrived back from New York, that awful Jasmine Buckley has been in Brodie's every night."

"Has she?" I felt myself stiffen as my mind flicked back to the last time I remembered seeing them together. How he appeared uncomfortable in her presence. "How do you know?"

"I've been working extra shifts for him . . . y'know . . . to help out."

I let out a sigh. "I see."

"Sorry. I shouldn't have said anything . . . it's just been bugging me, that's all."

"No. You're fine." I implored. "I guess that's the trouble with long-distance relationships. You just never know who's chasing after your man."

"I hope you're not upset with me for saying . . ." she said.

"I'm not Carmen." I declared. "If anything, you're just helping to clarify things for me."

"Please don't tell him I said something," she said.

"I promise you I won't," I reassured her.

I heard Carmen blow out a sigh of relief. I guessed the news of Jasmine had been bugging her for quite some time.

"OK. Before we get back to business . . . I have one question," I said.

"Go on?"

"Is there history between them?" I braced myself for the answer.

"Yes. Unfortunately, there is!"

"Fuck! Sorry, shouldn't have said that."

"You're OK. You're entitled to be annoyed. Let me see . . . it was waaay back, way before he met his wife. I think they may have dated back in high school. You know . . . nothing serious."

"Right. That's all I need to know. Thanks Carmen. Now email me over the sales figures please."

I fumed for the remainder of the afternoon. I guessed there was something about that awful Jasmine. The way she navigated herself in between Pat and I for the photos in the San Francisco store.

I switched on the sound system in the apartment and pulled out my trusty trolley bag. "Jasmine Buckley, you can have him."

"High school freakin sweethearts . . . yeuch!" I mumbled.

I railed through the closet and pulled out a selection of dresses from my wardrobe. Even If I can't work at the shows, I'm going to be on the sidelines cheering Jackson on.

I ignored Patrick's nightly text and instead sent a message to Jackson asking him to get me a seat reserved."

He responded straight away. "I have one for you on the sixth row."

I laughed. "Do I need to bring the binoculars?"

"Very funny sweetheart . . . just bring your gorgeous self," he said.

I threw the phone down on top of the bed, just as it pinged. I glanced at the name--it was from Patrick. I chose to ignore and poured myself another glass of wine.

Amy Winehouse belted out *Back to Black* as I sat on the armchair, tapping my fingers on the armrest, drinking the last residues of red wine.

I stared at the phone.

To hell with him.

CHAPTER THIRTEEN

Widow's Wardrobe

The day before I was due to fly out to London, I got up from my vanity table and searched in my closet for a suitable outfit to wear to the courthouse. I laughed at myself as I perused my widow's wardrobe complete with 12 black non-identical dressed all lined up. Rick was right, I had to do something about that situation . . . inject some colour into it . . . but how? My eyes wandered in the direction of colourful bags and purses all neatly displayed on three shelves. There were rows and rows of mostly unworn shoes lined up under the handbags.

I chose a 1960s silhouette dress that skimmed just below the knee and matched it with a high gloss red Kelly bag and a pair of scarlet Louboutin's. Then I rummaged around in my vanity for a va voom red lipstick that matched the bag and shoes. To finish, I chose my warm black vintage swing coat to go over the top of the outfit.

Who knew that so much effort went into going to court to have divorce papers finalized?

I sent a message to Rick.

"What are you wearing?"

"What's up?" he replied.

"We're going to the courthouse, you idiot!"

In typical Rick fashion, he had forgotten all about our court date.

I didn't know whether to laugh or cry.

How did I even end up with him?

I sat down on the floor and set about re-arranging my shoes. I had nothing better to do with my time. That was when I spotted a familiar-looking book stuck in behind a suitcase. I reached in, pulled it out and dusted it off.

How I used to lean on you.

I smiled to myself as I practiced my old ritual of opening the yellow book up at a random page.

The book flew open at: "She remembered who she was, and the game changed--Lalah Deliah."

I love this!

My spirit soared.

I sat there and let the words sink in, as my memory revved up into top gear.

Who are you Willow? What do you really, really want?

I sat on the floor and hugged my knees. I leaned against the wall under the hemlines of the black dresses as the memories danced in and out of my mind, reminding me of how far I had come.

Only a few short years ago, there I stood behind my makeup counter, my life going nowhere. That was the day Rick had wandered into my life, I laughed to myself. It hadn't taken long for things to go south. There had been no substance to our relationship. I was escaping something and apparently so was he--Isabella.

I knew then what I had to do. I took out my phone and called Patrick. No text messages, no opportunities for crossed wires, this time I was going to have a proper conversation with him and tell how I really felt about him.

Patrick picked up straight away.

"Hi!" His voice sounded warm and husky. "How are you?"

"I . . . er . . . I'm doing great." I paused before blurting out, "I'm getting divorced this afternoon."

Patrick was silent for a moment as if trying to decide how best to respond.

"And how do you feel about that?" he asked.

"Happy . . . mostly." I twirled my hair in my finger as I spoke, glancing at the quote on the open page. "It's just that... I remembered who I was." I said.

"Oh! I didn't realise you were struggling with memory loss." Patrick chuckled a little. But my voice had a serious tone to it.

"No. Seriously . . . I just remembered who I am and why I'm here." I stated. The butterflies in my stomach were doing their usual backflips as the palms of my hands sweated.

"Oh?" He sounded like he didn't know how to respond. "That sounds . . . um . . . serious."

"I just realized something Patrick . . . I'm here . . . on this big, beautiful planet . . . to be happy." The words tumbled out of my mouth before I had the chance to censor them. The heat rose in my face as it dawned on me there was no going back now.

Patrick's voice was loaded with hesitancy. "Are you OK, Willow . . . have you been drinking? Are you upset over your boss?"

I grew frustrated. "No! Yes! I mean I'm supposed to be happy, Patrick . . . and I'm not."

Patrick attempted to placate. "Look I know you've been through some tough times . . ."

I summoned up the courage to say what I truly wanted to say.

"I'm happy when I'm with you." I blurted.

There was silence on the other end of the phone.

"Patrick? Are you there? Can you hear me?" I called. The line went dead.

The blood ran cold in my veins as I stared at my phone.

"Patrick! How fucking dare you!" I shouted out.

I let out a yell of exasperation then threw the phone at the wall. It bounced off the wall and landed on top of the book.

I stood up and stamped my feet, not caring about the tenants in the apartment below.

"I'm done," I said to no-one in particular, and picked up the phone and texted Jackson.

"Meet me off the flight please. I arrive on the BA flight at 8am tomorrow."

CHAPTER FOURTEEN

Bittersweet Symphony

It had been over two years since I set foot on British soil. The aroma of petrol infiltrated my nostrils as Jackson and I stepped into a black cab outside Heathrow Airport.

"Pollution! Don't you just love it!" I laughed as I cozied up beside him in the back seat of the cab.

"How was the flight?" he asked, looking in his man bag for some concealer and foundation. He went to work straight away, fixing my eyeliner which was difficult considering the number of potholes in the roads.

"Oh well, you know--overnight flights are always uncomfortable." Then I remembered that he had flown in First Class with Carlotta on the way back home.

Jackson tutted in a superior way, "Not in First Class, darling, you get to sleep the whole way home." He chuckled as he recalled his arrival in the UK, "you then get woken up and presented with a bottle of Bolly for breakfast."

"Shut up!" I whacked him on the arm, "I don't want to hear anymore."

"So, how's it been with Carlotta . . . non-stop partying I guess?" I asked, as he pinched my eyebrow up into an arch.

"You could say that, but she's also a bit of a hard taskmistress if you know what I mean?"

"No. I don't know what you mean." I said. I clearly had no clue what he was insinuating.

"God, Willow. How do you get through the day?"

I furrowed my brow and shook my head. I really was clueless.

Jackson exhaled and drew me one of his know it all looks. "She likes to work the team really hard, has her favourites…you know the way it goes."

The penny dropped. "Ah! I see."

"Yes." He ran his hand through his hair and checked his reflection in the mirror. "

"You never know what version you're getting…she's like the wind."

"Oooh!" I shivered. "I didn't think she was like that."

"C'mon . . . she has oodles of fame and wealth and can behave however she wants." He threw himself back into the seat and stared out of the window.

"That's a pity." I clasped my hands on my knees and looked out the window at the views of Hounslow as we made our way towards Isleworth.

"She's having the time of her life . . . I guess." Jackson stated then turned his attention to me. "Just got to be careful around her, don't piss her off. Proper narcissist, she is."

"What about you and that Brad Brodie guy?" he asked.

"You mean Patrick Brodie?" I shook my head. "There's nothing to tell, really."

Any sensation of happiness I felt at seeing Jackson again began to dissipate.

"It's too difficult. He's got a young daughter . . . and she doesn't like me and . . ." I looked out the window again. "I called him yesterday to tell him how I really felt about him but the line went dead."

"What?" Jackson looked shocked. "No! Don't believe it. There must be some explanation . . . a fault on the line or something? No?"

Now it was Jackson's turn to look out the window. "That sucks!" he said, "and he was hot! A big step up from Rick and Jake."

I wacked him on the arm again. "You just can't help yourself, can you?"

Jackson shrugged. "Just trying to lighten things up . . . what about the divorce?"

I leaned into my green Kate Spade bag and pulled out a bunch of papers. "All done."

"So, you're officially Willow Campbell again?!"

"Willow Jade Campbell." I stated, with a certain amount of flair. It was an enormous relief to finally be separated from Rick.

"How's that going to affect your legal status?"

I looked out the window at the hustle and bustle of city streets. "I got my Green Card a few months ago," I turned and smiled at him.

"C'mere a minute, lady."

Jackson leaned over with a tissue. "You've got some specks of red on your teeth."

"Can't take you bloody anywhere." Jackson mocked as he set about blotting my lipstick.

"Got a question to ask." his expression changed.

"Go on." I urged.

"Now." He paused. "Don't take this wrong way and don't get upset with me."

"Uh oh. Don't know if I like the sound of this."

"Did you marry Rick for the Green Card?" He cocked an eyebrow and stared at me.

A sensation of fury and indignation built up inside me.

"No! I bloody well did not." I sat back in the back seat of the taxi and folded my arms in indignation.

Then I turned to look at him. "And how dare you even insinuate that."

"OK. OK. Calm down. I just needed to ask, that's all." He glared.

He had hurt my feelings. "I thought you knew me better than this, Jackson. You've insulted me."

"I'm sorry, Willow. I'm only asking what other people are thinking."

"Well, if you're trying to make things better between us then you're failing . . . miserably."

"Christ Almighty, stop being so touchy." Jackson threw himself back against the leather seat and folded his arms, as we continued on in silence.

My thoughts raced.

Is that what everyone thinks of me? Really?

Homeland Security certainly thought so.

I sighed heavily and broke the silence between us. "If you really want to know the truth, I did love Rick. I really thought we could make it."

Jackson came out of his huffy mood. "Sorry Willow," he mumbled under his breath. "Sorry for disrespecting you."

But the damage had been done. I felt tarnished.

"We're almost there," he said. He brightened up to jolly me along but I just couldn't get into the spirit of things, not after that last comment. I was tired and jet-lagged. All I wanted was to have a shower and go straight to bed. Fall asleep in a nice, cozy narrow little British bed.

"You're gonna love this place," he said. "They have Cath Kidston matching bedding and wallpaper. I chose the cabbage patch bedroom for my favourite girl."

I had to hand it to Jackson. He always knew how to drag me out of a mood . . . knew the right things to say.

The taxi pulled onto the gravel driveway of a white-painted Georgian house near the River Thames. He paid the driver, collected my luggage from the boot of the car then put his arm in mine and walked me towards the entrance to the hotel.

As we waited at reception, standing in line behind another couple, Jackson whispered, "I know just what you need." He pulled a silver flask out of his jacket pocket and handed it to me.

"Pink Gin!" he beamed. "Thought you might be in the mood to celebrate." The memory of Patrick doing the same thing that night at the winery came flooding back, causing my mood to descend once more.

I fell into his arms and hugged him tight. No matter how bad circumstances in my life were, life always seemed brighter with Jackson around.

We climbed up two narrow flights of stairs towards the room on the second floor. Jackson put the key in the lock and opened the door to reveal a chic interior.

"Looks way better in real life than what it does in the photos." He scanned the accommodation and plonked my suitcase down on a little sage green velvet footstool. He was right. The vibrant cabbage patch wallpaper cheered me up. Over to the side of the room was a single, white-painted wrought-iron bedstead with the comfiest-looking single bed I have ever seen. The cabbage patch duvet looked sumptuous. The pillowslips were made from the finest Egyptian cotton. The window looked out over the gravel driveway. In front of the window stood a cast iron claw foot bathtub on its very own platform.

I shook my head and smiled at Jackson. "This is just," I sighed, "so bloody marvellous." I sat down on top of the bed and let Jackson get to work, hanging up my coat in the wardrobe then drawing the curtain so that I could go to sleep.

"Over there in the ensuite, you've got a rainfall shower." He peered in to look then called back, "all white marble, my love!"

"Thank you! You're such a sweetheart." I giggled, as I began to relax into my surroundings. I opened the flask and took a swig of the gin then smacked my lips. "Good. That'll help me fall asleep."

Jackson checked his watch. "Right. I'd better be off," he said. "Carlotta and Daphne will be waiting for me over at The Strand."

That got my attention. "The Strand, you said?"

Jackson touched the side of his nose with his finger, and chuckled.

"Wait a wee minute . . . whose makeup are you doing?" I asked.

Jackson burst into laughter. "I signed an NDA, so I can't discuss it with ya!"

"Bloody hell, just what are you up to?"

"You'll find out soon enough." Jackson pulled back the duvet and indicated for me to get in. "I'll be back for you at 5:00 pm," he said. "That'll give you plenty of time to get some rest before we go out tonight." He looked over at the claw-foot tub. "I would suggest you start running that at 3:00 pm, it takes an age to draw."

"Have you stayed here before?" I asked, intrigued as to how he had acquired so much intimate knowledge about the inner workings of the hotel.

"Yeah," he beamed. "Why do you think I chose it for you?" He walked over towards the window and pointed out. "Over there is one of the best pubs in this neck of the woods and just around the corner is Princess Diana's old gym. Plus, you're ten minutes from Richmond High Street, so you've got it all going on." He smiled, proud of his choice in accommodation. He checked his watch again. "Right. I'm going now." He blew me a kiss and shut the door behind him.

As Jackson's energy departed, I was aware of the silence in the room. The room was fragranced with a delightful combination of lavender and ylang-ylang filling the atmosphere with a soothing and relaxing ambiance. I checked out the bathroom amenities and saw they had the Cowshed brand on display. I nodded my approval. This place was exactly to my liking: elegant Georgian cheekbones with high ceilings and ornate flourishes.

I skipped having a shower. Instead, I opened my trolley bag and pulled out my comfiest PJs. I walked over to the huge windows and pulled the heavy, black velvet curtains shut tight. It had started snowing outside. I threw myself into a heap on the narrow bed and pulled the heavy duvet over me. My phone was pinging like crazy but I chose to ignore the constant stream of messages coming in. The alarm was set for 3:00 pm. I still felt gutted about my short-lived relationship with Patrick. As I tried to shut thoughts of Patrick out of my mind, the welcome arrival of jet-lag enveloped me and I went out like a light.

***

Bathed, dressed and ready to explore the city, I awaited Jackson's arrival in the 'great room' downstairs. The journey back to the UK had left me with a huge appetite, as I looked at the menu, there was no doubt in my mind--I had to order the English High Tea which consisted of a tradi-tional cake stand full to overflowing with dainty sandwiches with the crusts cut off. The waitress brought me a fine white china teapot filled to the brim with what could only be described as 'builder's tea.'"

I took a sip. "By God, that's good." I smacked my lips and got stuck into the cream-laden scones and jam. How I had missed this very British mid-afternoon ritual.

At 3:30 pm, Jackson trundled into the room and indicated for me to join him in the lobby. I left a tip for the waitress and joined him outside in the driveway, where a black London cab was waiting for us. Inside the cab, a woman sat in the back seat.

Jackson introduced us. "Willow. This is Daphne."

I smiled at her and offered her my hand as I climbed in. "Pleased to meet you." I smiled.

She scanned me from top to toe, her expression unchanged as she took a drag on her cigarette then flicked the ash out of the window. She held total disregard for the 'no-smoking' signs that were plastered on the win-dows of the cab.

For a brief second, I thought she resembled Siouxsie from Siouxsie and the Banshees. Her jet-black mane was dyed purple at the roots and her gothic makeup concealed the person below. She wore skin-tight PVC trousers, a black leather biker's jacket and a pair of spiked ¾ boots. I noticed her right hand had a henna tattoo of an indecipherable language and there was me dressed like I was going to meet the Queen.

Jackson called over to the driver and asked him to take us to The

Strand.

He called back to us. "You sure mate? Don't think they'll let the likes of her in," he smirked.

I tried to conceal a smile as Daphne drew me a look and told the driver to fuck off and mind his own business, then she turned her attention on me.

Her accent was northern English. I couldn't quite place it exactly.

"So, you've decided to come back to the homeland?" she asked.

I wondered who had given her that impression. "No. I'm only here to launch the UK boutique and then I have to fly back to New York."

Daphne smacked her gum then thought for a moment or two. She turned to Jackson. "That's not what you told me?"

He looked uncomfortable. "What did you say to Daphne about me?" I asked.

Jackson looked like he had been caught up in a lie. "I . . . um . . . told her you might like an opportunity to work the shows with me." He stared at me as he pressed his boot on top of my shoe."

"Well . . . that's,"

Jackson pressed harder.

"Well of course I would love to have the opportunity to work the shows with you guys . . . if that were even possible?"

Jackson released some of the pressure off my foot.

"That'll depend on how well you get on tonight . . . at The Strand." She smacked her gum in her mouth and continued to stare at me.

"So, what exactly is happening tonight?" I asked, looking at Jackson.

"I told you I had to sign an NDA--a non-disclosure agreement."

I nodded. "Yeah, you did."

"Well, that means I can't talk about it." He placed his hands on his knees and stared at me. Now I was more confused than before.

Daphne took a hip flask out of her pocket, opened it, took a swig then passed a pill to Jackson. He did the same as Daphne, then passed a pill and the flask to me.

"What's this?" I looked on horrified.

He patted me on the knee and smiled. "Just a little something to relax you before you meet . . . Oops! I nearly gave the game away." Both he and Daphne laughed hard as I gripped onto my Kelly bag.

I drew him a disapproving glance and looked out the window.

God, what has he got me into?

Forty-five minutes later, the three of us passed through security at The Strand. Daphne caused a bit of a stir with the amount of metal she had on her person. She was clearly not happy at having to take her boots off and pad through security with her Minnie Mouse socks on.

Maybe under all that menacing outerwear, she's really a little softy at heart.

Next up was Jackson. I noticed he drank the last dregs of his alcohol of choice before placing the empty hip flask in the big tray.

The more I saw of him, the more he worried me.

Next up was me. I emptied the contents of my Kelly bag into the tray, took off my shoes and walked in my bare feet. I was glad I had found time to get myself a pedicure. It was a new habit I had acquired living in New York. My feet were ice-cold.

All three of us were allowed to put our shoes back on and make our way towards a very grand hallway.

"Where are we going now?" I asked.

"You'll see in a minute." Jackson put his arm around me as we walked behind Daphne. I could tell she was clearly in her element as she greeted suited men and women. Everyone appeared to know who she was . . . everyone except for me.

When she was far enough in front of us and out of earshot, I stopped Jackson in her tracks.

"Now, tell me what is going on." I demanded, staring at him hard.

"OK. This is the dress rehearsal for the London Fashion Week shows. In that room ahead of us, the world's leading supermodels are having their makeup done and are being fitted for their outfits." He beamed proudly.

"Are you on the team?" I asked, my heart was racing.

"I am." He hugged me tight.

I was proud as hell for my buddy. It was every makeup artist's dream to work the shows.

I stepped away from him and ran my hands up and down his arms. "So, you're not going to be my manager?"

I answered the question for him. "I guess not!" I shrugged as we laughed and smiled. It wasn't a great revelation to me. Jackson's career had just gone stratospheric.

"Do you need me to wash your brushes for you?" I joked, as we stepped into a grand room full of beautiful male and female models, designers, hairdressers and other makeup artists.

Jackson looked over at me, his eyes crinkled as he spoke, "Welcome to my world, Willow."

I watched on as Jackson was whisked away by Daphne and a bunch of her very glamorous cohorts. I felt silly standing there in my demure out-fit, standing out like a sore thumb in comparison to many of the avant-garde types all around me. Everyone there had a job or some important function to perform to make sure the show went off without a hitch: de-signers scurried around with pins in their mouths as they instructed their assistants and models on how to wear their outfits, while the team of makeup artists and hairdressers got to work creating iconic hairstyles and painting the faces of their models.

I couldn't help wondering what Patrick was doing right now.

Stop it, Willow! Pay attention! You're backstage at the shows and thinking about an unobtainable man . . . what's the matter with you, woman!

Jackson interrupted my thoughts and pulled me by the hand into the busy crowd, rushing me towards his model. I recognized her straight away . . . it was The Muse! My muse from the New York Artistry

Competition.

She took a long, drawn puff on her cigarette as Jackson introduced us.

"Willow!" she gasped, hugging me while dropping cigarette ash on my bare arm, but I was overwhelmed that she had remembered my name. "How the devil are you? I bloody knew we would meet again." She air-kissed me on both cheeks while Jackson looked on from the sidelines. "Are you working the shows too?" she asked, "Please say yes!" she clutched onto my wrist.

I shook my head. "No. I'm just here to support this guy." I looked over at him with pride.

Is he blushing? Surely not.

"Jackson, why didn't you get Willow on the team?" The Muse looked indignant.

"It's OK, really. I'm here on business. Got a shop to open . . . a little pop-up store on Brewer Street."

The muse sat on the makeup chair while Jackson got to work on prepping her skin. "Tell me more . . ." she asked.

A half-hour must have passed as I regaled stories about everything that happened since the last time we met. The Muse listened, while I talked. I hadn't had such a captive audience in a long time, not since Mrs. G. had passed or since the time I spent with Patrick in San Francisco.

"Wait a minute . . . so the goal is to buy back D'Arcy's Department Store with the proceeds of three pop-up stores?"

I could tell she was doing mental calculations in her head as I spoke.

She stubbed out her cigarette in the ashtray and scratched her head. "I hate to say it, Willow, but it sounds like the old lady left you with an insurmountable task."

I felt stupid. "I know." I shook my head.

"Oh! I didn't mean to make you feel despondent," she sympathised. "You just need to find some backers."

"What do you mean?" I asked.

The Muse pulled away from Jackson and turned around to face me straight on.

"You need to find a big name that can come on board and help you out."

"Right." I said, trying my best to regain some kind of composure. "I'll get right on it."

The Muse reached into her purse that was placed on top of the makeup table. She opened it and pulled out a white card.

I read the inscription. "Chivas Bros. Accountants."

"Yes. Send your pitch for investment to that address and I'll get Charles to look it over on my behalf."

I stared at the card, then at The Muse.

"What?" I gasped.

"I'm not just a pretty face, Willow." She laughed, then took another drag on her cigarette.

***

I woke up the next morning with the biggest hangover I had experienced in a very long time. My head pounded as I reached over to the bedside table in search of a box of aspirin. That's when I noticed Jackson lying on a heap on the floor, fully-clothed and clutching my dressing gown as a blanket.

He opened one eye, gave me a half smile then went back to sleep while I took in my surroundings. I recognized the distinctive wallpaper and realized that we were back in the hotel that I had checked into the day before. Memories of the night before came flooding back at breakneck speed. I scrambled around for my bag and pulled out my purse. The white card was intact, minus a red wine stain.

"So, I didn't dream it." I said out loud to no-one in particular. "She really did give me her card."

I looked at my reflection in the mirror as I gripped onto it. A huge smile crept across my face as I remembered that one of the world's top supermodels was vaguely interested in helping me buy back D'Arcy's Department Store from the receiver.

"Shall I order coffee for us?" I asked and made my way towards the bathroom.

I heard him mumble 'Yes' as he stumbled into my bed and pulled the duvet over his head. I looked at the clock, the shows were due to start in five hours' time and Jackson was in a terrible state. I heard him mumble and groan while I wracked my brains trying to conjure up a potent hang-over cure that could get him fit and ready in time for the shows.

The Room service attendant arrived and placed a huge silver platter down on the table. Once he was gone, I set everything out on the plates and poured out two cups of coffee. As I ate my 'Full English' breakfast, I listened to him snoring. I noticed a bottle of pills lying on the carpet and reached out to pick them up. I researched the brand name, shocked to find out they were for depression.

My Jackson? Depressed?

I saw him stir under the duvet and quickly placed the pills back in the spot where he had left them.

He must have had such a hard time going home and starting from scratch all over again.

I shook my head.

Can't have been easy for him.

I made a mental note to talk about the pills with him later, but first I had to get him ready to perform at the shows.

***

I showered and dressed and threw on some makeup to help disguise the effects of my hangover, which was growing worse as time went on. When I came out of the bathroom, Jackson was snoring loudly from under the duvet. I looked at the time. We had to be back at the shows for 2:30 pm, in order to prep the models for the runway.

I called to Jackson, but he didn't hear me.

I went over and nudged him, gently at first but then more vigorously. "For God's sake, wake up, will you?"

"Leave me alone," he said.

I grew angry with him. "Get up! This is one of the biggest days of your career and look at the state of you."

Jackson pulled down the duvet to reveal his face. He was a terrible colour. So, so pale with a touch of green, or maybe it was the dim light in the room. I don't know but he looked awful.

"Do you want me to bring you some coffee? It's still warm." I said.

He pulled the duvet back over his face and groaned lightly. I turned my back on him for a second just as he got up and made a sprint for the bathroom.

The sounds that came out of there were indescribable.

"This is not good," I said to myself as I checked the time again. My phone was buzzing. It was Daphne.

"Hello, Willow? How's Jackson?" she asked, her voice was pitched high as she spoke.

I looked back towards the bathroom and heard more violent retching.

"Um . . . he's not good."

"Shit!" she screeched. "There were some dodgy pills going around last night at the party." She paused, "I think he may have taken one." She declared, awaiting my response.

"Yes. I'm going to have to have a talk with him about that." I stated, sounding like I was his mother.

There was another long pause on the phone. "You do makeup, don't you? He told me you both worked together in New York. He said you weren't as good as him but you could still do a good job."

Oh no, lady. You don't. I'm not being put in that position. This is Jackson's big day.

The retching continued on in the background as the seriousness of the situation unfolded in front of me.

Daphne was growing more agitated. "Look if it's the money . . . we'll pay you," she stated impatiently.

"It's not the money." I shook my head. "I just can't." I lowered my voice, "This is his big opportunity and I'm not going to take it away from him.

"Look. Willow. I don't give a shit about all that nonsense. I'm one makeup artist down for the shows and I'm asking you to fill in for him. If you don't. He's out of the team."

"What? You can't blackmail me like that." I shouted. "That's not fair and you know it."

I had tried to warm to Daphne the previous night but there was just something about her that I didn't quite like and I couldn't put my finger on it. Now I knew why I didn't like her.

At that moment, Jackson stumbled out of the bathroom with a towel wrapped around him. He whisked past me and fell back into the bed.

"I'm dying," he said.

I covered the handset with my hand and called over to him. "You're not dying, you just took a dodgy pill. Now go to sleep."

"He's in very bad shape." I said to Daphne. I also knew what I had to do but I wasn't going to hand it to her on a plate. She needed me.

"OK. What's the latest you need me there by?"

I heard Daphne exhale with relief. "2.45 pm and no later. The show starts at 4:00pm." She paused. "Thank you, Willow. Because of you, Jackson gets to stay in the team, but if he does this again, he's out on his ass. Maybe you can get the message across to him."

"I'll do my best."

***

Daphne stood waiting for me at the entrance. As soon as I stepped out of the cab, she whisked me through security and led me towards the same grand room we had been in the previous evening before the party.

The Muse sat on her chair, smoking a cigarette and drinking from a can of coke. Her face lit up when she saw me walk towards her. "What? No Jackson?"

I nodded.

The Muse gave me a knowing smile but said nothing.

"OK . . . let's get this show on the road." I disinfected my hands and began to set the brushes out the way I liked them.

I couldn't quite believe that I was getting a second chance to work on the exquisite face of one of the world's leading supermodels. Daphne handed me a makeover card and gave me directions on the specific colours she wanted me to apply. The look was pure drama: lots of blacks, greys, purple and silver. Her hair was pulled up in a tight ballet bun, revealing perfect contours and a subtle elegance. It had been over a year since I last did her makeup, and yet she had hardly aged at all.

The time passed quickly as we talked about what we had both done in the time since we last met. Other lesser-known models milled around, casting envious looks in our direction as I continued to work on her face. My nerves had been kicked into high gear but I couldn't let them get the better of me.

"Almost done," I whispered.

She had been on her phone the whole time, talking to her son and making arrangements with her friends for dinner later in the evening.

As I applied the last layer of lipstick to her rosebud-shaped lips, she looked up at me. "Do you want to join us for dinner after the show, Willow? said The Muse. "We're going to the Smokehouse."

"Aww . . . that's so kind of you, but I have to get back to Jackson . . . see how he's feeling," I said.

"You're a good friend. He's lucky to have you," she said.

"Yes, I'm lucky to have him too." I replied.

If truth be known, I was dreading going back to Jackson.

How will he take the news that I took his place at London Fashion Week?

When the music began thumping out of the loudspeakers and all the models were lined up backstage, I packed up my brushes and tidied up the table before checking my phone. My heart stopped for a second as I checked my messages. Jackson had tried to phone me.

I didn't feel like I wanted to call him back. Instead, I placed the phone in my bag and sidled off out the back door and out into the snowy, dark street. I pulled the collar of my jacket up tight around my neck. I wasn't dressed for the type of weather we were having but I couldn't care less.

I've just achieved my lifetime's ambition so why do I feel so hollow inside?

I stood at a bus stop and watched on as a group of models left the building and jumped into taxis that would take them to their next destination. While I had just turned down a dinner invitation with a supermodel and her friends. I kicked a loose stone and stared at the bus timetable hoping there would be one soon . . . one that would take me back to my hotel room in Isleworth.

Never mind. You did good. You've got a shop to open tomorrow.

CHAPTER FIFTEEN

What's It All About, Willow?

It was a frosty morning and the streets and trees were covered in snow. It was unusual for London to have a snowfall like this. I put the key into the door of the boutique on Brewer Street and held my breath.

Please God . . . let this work!

After much nudging and twisting, I opened the door to hear the alarm go off. I followed the instructions on my little bit of paper and rushed to the back room where the alarm console was attached to a wall. I put in the correct number sequence and breathed a sigh of relief.

OK. That's that little problem out of the way.

I looked around. It would be another hour before the candidates would begin to line up, so I had some time to get myself acquainted with my new surroundings. I filled the kettle with some London tap water and filled a cafetiere with some ground coffee left behind by the previous tenants.

I knew how to spot for signs of mice and rats and yes, there were the usual traps lying around in obvious places.

At least I knew the problem was being attended too. I could deal with it better that way.

I stepped out onto the shop floor and took in my surroundings. The builders and carpenters had done a great job at getting the store outfitted in the Plane Jane Beauty brand style. The interior was not too different to the San Franciscan store. All those zoom calls with the designer and construction team had worked wonders. I made a mental note to send the designer a bouquet of flowers to thank her.

I took a sip of my coffee and looked at my phone. Apart from a message from George wishing me well, my heart missed a beat as I realized that this time I would be on my own. There would be no more annoying text messages and insane demands from Mrs. G. This time around I was going to have to use my own judgment and hope for the best. I scanned the phone to see if I had perhaps missed a message from Patrick. Zero. Nothing. Nada.

To hell with him. That's the last time I ever wear my heart on my sleeve. All it does is scare men away.

Jackson had promised to show up at the end of his gig but I didn't bank on that either. I guessed that once today's runway shows were over, he would continue to go out partying with the models.

I turned on the sound system while I got to grips with instructions on how to use the till system.

"Shouldn't be too difficult", I coached myself, as I navigated the till screen. All the Plane Jane Beauty products had been inputted into the system so everything should be straightforward.

I was deep in concentration as the bar to *The First Time Ever I Saw Your Face* by Roberta Flack played. I stopped in my tracks as I listened to the lyrics. A tear trickled down my cheek as the emotion of the words got the better of me.

Pull yourself together Willow. Said the voice. *Now is not the time for emotions.* But I couldn't stop the tears. My life was whizzing by at breakneck speed and every time I thought I wanted something in life, saw out an ambition . . . I realized that the ambition didn't really mean anything at all. It was just a thing. A goal. And I had no-one special to share my wins with . . . in that case it was all pointless. London Fashion Week had been pointless, opening the San Francisco store had been pointless. Mrs. G. was gone. Jackson was heading off on his own path, my parents were long time passed away and everything seemed pointless.

The next song that came on was Dionne Warwick singing *What's It all About Alfie?* Another of my favourites. I input some information into the computer system and mocked up a transaction.

Bloody hell! Can't even do a simple thing like that. Come on, Willow. Get yourself together.

I typed out an email to Carmen asking for her assistance with setting up the candidates in the system prior to interviewing them. I typed as fast as I could while making mental calculations in my head regarding the time zone difference. *Will she even be awake?* I searched in Google-- what's the time difference between London and San Francisco? It was 10:30 am in London and only 2:30 am in San Francisco.

This is no good, she'll be asleep. Shit! What am I going to do?

I turned the music down low so that I could concentrate better.

As the notes on the piano tinkled, I grew more and more harassed.

The door went. I carried on looking at my screen and typed while I called out, "Sorry, we're not open yet."

"That's a pity."

I looked up from the screen. Patrick stood in front of me. He walked towards me, his hands slouched in his pockets.

"I was hoping you could do something with this two o'clock shadow." He pointed to the side of his face. "It's a long way to fly from 'Frisco."

I threw my pen down on the counter and ran to him, throwing my arms around his neck as he hugged me tight. I buried my head into his shoulder as I inhaled his musky, masculine scent. He ran his hands through my hair and kissed me softly at first, then with hunger.

In between our kisses he managed to speak a few words. "This is crazy. Us being apart like this. I can't stand to be away from you."

My heart beat faster in my chest as I reciprocated. "Nothing means anything anymore without you. I need you."

When we eventually pulled apart and stared at each other. "What are we going to do about this situation?" He laced his arms around my back, pulling me in closer. "I can't sleep. I can't think straight." He twirled a lock of my hair in his finger. "I've lost my appetite. I need you in my life."

"Same here." I gasped, pulling him closer and burying my face in his chest. "Everything seems pointless without you." I looked over his shoulder. "Did you bring Coco with you?"

He shook his head. "No. I couldn't take her out of school. My mom's looking after her."

"That's nice." I smiled, relieved that I had him all to myself.

"How long are you here for?" I asked.

"For as long as it takes to win you back." He looked shamefaced. "That night you phoned me and told me how you truly felt . . . it was all too much, I couldn't deal with . . ."

I placed my finger up at his lips to shush him up. "You don't need to say anything." I shook my head gently. "You're here now. That's all that matters to me."

Patrick swept in for another kiss as the doorbell went once more.

We parted to look over and see two women and a man standing at the door.

"Are you Mrs. Campbell?" The tall young lady asked.

I swiped a glance at Patrick and smiled. "Yes. I am. How can I help you?"

She looked back at the other two who were standing in the doorway. "Yes, guys, we're in the right place."

I held Patrick's hand in mine, stared into his green eyes and mouthed the words, ". . . and so are we."

To be continued . . .

Acknowledgements

Well, I've heard of the 'second album' being difficult, I had no idea that this also applied to writing the sequel in a series, so in that case, I want to give huge thanks to Amy Tipton @FeralGirlBooks for her Developmental Editing and keeping me on track with 'Willow.' Moving to a new country halfway through the process did not help matters either! But battered and bruised, we got there in the end!

And then we handed over the reins to Stephen Joyce for Line Editing, thanks Stephen for making Willow such a 'smooth' read.

Magic happens when you see the book cover for the first time, and everything finally falls into place. I'm so lucky to have such a talented husband on hand to create this standout artwork.

And to Socciones Editoria Digitale for bringing the whole package together and launching my books into the world.

***

Another huge shout-out to my family and friends (you know who you are!) for continually supporting me throughout this mad, magical writing career of mine and to *Suzy Wong for supplying the prosecco and giggles.*

And to my readers who read and supplied valuable feedback: Angela Cairns, Anne McKenna, Caroline Farry, Caroline McBride, Catherine Muir, Christian Linton, Jane McCormack, Jessica Wagstaff, Katie McBride, Janet Oetterer, Kristine Humber, Laura Donnan, Mary McKenzie, Morag Morrison, Sue Tate, Susan Charleston-Daisley and Toinette Campbell.

Finally, to my Mum, Llorraine, Isabel and Susie for being always available to chat.

***

Once again, there's wonderful music in this book. I'll never forget Film Producer Gary Goldman's advice to write to music. I took this to heart, so my boys know more about Burt Bacharach, The Mamas and Papas and Dionne Warwick than most kids from their generation — thanks Gary!

And to all the lovely new friends I made in my first year in Canada. You had no idea that I was about to land on your doorstep — thanks for making me feel so welcome and for embracing my work.

Passing the baton to K.N. Kaudel, my fellow writer and colleague, it was fab to have another writer to talk to during the long, dark days of my first Canadian winter. I can't wait to see what you do!

Finally, a note to my nieces Molly, Freya, Laura, Katie, Emma, Sophie, Cherylynn and Haley — **'Be Fabulous!'**

If you're reading this and you enjoyed 'Willow', please consider leaving a review online.

When I first wrote 'Warpaint' as a film screenplay, I had no idea it would turn into a trilogy. I've loved developing the characters over time and I'm not ready to let them go just yet. I'll aim to get the third book out by Christmas 2023.

In the meantime, you can find me on:

Instagram here: @J.J.Maya

Tik Tok here: @J.J.Mayaauthor

Link to Book 1 in the series (USA): Amazon.com/dp/B085HX12SV
Link to Book 1 in the series (UK): Amazon.co.uk/dp/B085HX12SV

Sign up to my Beauty Shop Girl newsletter here:
mailchi.mp/55d48b70359c/jj-maya

I'm also on Goodreads and Bookbub.

I can't tell you how thrilled and delighted I am to have you as a reader, and I want to thank you for taking a chance on me.

J.J.Maya